I0685474

Bride by Proxy

by

Lori Power

McGuire Series, Book 2

This is a work of fiction. Names, characters, places, and incidents are either the product of the author's imagination or are used fictitiously, and any resemblance to actual persons living or dead, business establishments, events, or locales, is entirely coincidental.

Bride by Proxy

Cover Art by *Debbie Taylor*

The Wild Rose Press, Inc.
PO Box 708
Adams Basin, NY 14410-0708
Visit us at www.thewildrosepress.com

Publishing History
First Edition, 2021
Trade Paperback ISBN 978-1-5092-3720-3
Digital ISBN 978-1-5092-3721-0

McGuire Series, Book 2
Published in the United States of America

Garrett controlled the sudden urge to set his father's letter aflame and pretend he'd never received the correspondence. Marry. As sole heir, his father expected him to return home to wed, produce legitimate sons, and continue the legacy. The matrimonial contract to join him with Beverly MacLeod had been drawn up before his own mother's death birthing a brother who lived only long enough to draw a few short breaths. This legal pact would finally fulfill a longstanding family alliance and bridge the McGuire name to one with a title to accompany and legitimize the wealth.

With their lands sharing a common border, the three MacLeod siblings and he had been tossed together as children, growing up as a school of fish—he and two sisters and their older brother, Brian, who'd become Garrett's lifelong friend. In fact, being of an age with Brian, he and Brian had both taken to the sea the same year, though on different vessels. Now Brian and he served together, Garrett as captain and Brian as his second.

Though he wasn't opposed to the family, marriage to Beverly held no attraction. Garrett shook his head, struggling to continue through the lengthy missive. Despite his best efforts, which in fact, represented little to no enthusiasm, he had no great regard for Beverly. True too, he remained in no doubt of her mutual disregard for him.

He rubbed the roughened stubble on his chin and tried to imagine his betrothed. Bollocks. Though it had been nigh on five years since he had last laid eyes upon her, he could not imagine she was anything more than the spoiled child she had been when he had last known her.

Praise for Lori Power

"*BLACK'S GOLD* is pure emotional escapism; a romance neatly wrapped up in a historical, swashbuckling piratical drama."

~Grant Leishman

~*~

"A well-paced plot and plenty of suspenseful moments…the McGuire Series is an ambitious and adventurous seafaring tale infused with romance."

~Lit Amri

~*~

"There's nothing that I didn't like about *BLACK'S GOLD*, and I gulped it down in one sitting. Anyone itching for a well-written seafaring adventure should check it out."

~Pikasho Deka

Dedication

Sometimes you know right away
but have to patiently wait for the right time.

Chapter One

1798

Garrett McGuire snapped the telescope closed yet continued to peer into the clear night sky. He breathed deeply of the salty brine. Both smell and taste tingled. The wind freshened off the inlet while he searched the stars. If asked, he couldn't say what he sought.

Answers?

Maybe.

To what questions?

What lay beyond what he couldn't see. He'd grown up understanding how to navigate according to the sun and stars, yet what and where he needed to go couldn't be answered in their knowing, steady charts.

He closed his eyes and drew another deep breath, and his heart mounted a bracing staccato. Her. A little girl not so little anymore by his measure of time, but to his boy's heart, now grown a man, she remained the keeper.

"The tide's right, Capt'in. Shall I light the signal?" Quartermaster Leonard Tippen asked as he climbed the steep stairs to the main deck. "All's quiet and no sign of patrols."

Reverie broken, Garrett's stare met Tippen's eye in acknowledgment. He followed this with a nod and gave the heavens one last sweeping glance. The stars were so bright they smiled down upon them unperturbed in their eternity like mini bonfires. Where were those celestial orbs when the *Isle Sky* had been fighting the spring storms crossing the Atlantic these last three weeks, he wondered. Fortunately, a new moon provided some cover tonight, and though the calm seas offered a welcomed reprieve along with a near tropical breeze, he would have preferred a slight fog this night to camouflage their presence in the open sea as they made their way into the secluded cove.

"One lantern, stern, three lifts," he ordered, turning his gaze toward the purple-shadowed land off the starboard bow. "These Americas are yet wild places. The British, despite their best efforts, have not fully secured this part of the world. Have the bosun's lad climb the mast to keep watch."

Because of his father's windfall while in command of his own ship, they now owned a fleet of merchant vessels, and his family continued their fortune through shipbuilding. The sea ran in his veins, his mother often said before her death, and true to this, Garrett had chosen the sea over a life of business despite his father's persistence that he consider the life of a gentleman. The unsettled whims of his mistress—the ocean—suited him fine. To appease her, ride her, live through her tantrums, and gratify her calm gave him purpose he could hardly articulate to anyone who did not share his affliction.

This choice did little to align him with his father's wishes, even though Garrett could see his father yearned for the comforts at sea despite remaining in England these last years since Garrett's mother's death.

But if he couldn't have "her," then he would stay in

2

the bosom of his mistress, who always welcomed him back.

His night-trained sight scanned the horizon, seeking the response. The sky was so clear that within minutes of the signal being relayed, the return beacon blossomed visible for all to see.

Hands loose behind his back, Garrett strode to the railing. "We move with the current. No need to fight what she freely gives." He turned to address the quartermaster, who then relayed the message through the chain of command. "We'll anchor in the usual position. Have the rowboats prepared to disembark. I'll go ashore with the first load."

"Aye Capt'in."

With a practiced bound, Garrett leapt into the boat and assumed his position. A few strokes brought their small party to the shore. Knees bent, feet braced against the sides, ahead of the rowers, he stood as it came aground on the pebbled sand. Suddenly the beach came alive with lamps flickering like fireflies, marking a path for the sailors. Stepping lightly, he jumped cleanly over the wooden side and strode through the lapping waves, taking little heed of the water reaching to the cuff of his stained leather boots.

A portly man, flanked by two tired-looking fellows, stood just to the side, lamps raised to his approach. "In these most dangerous times, it's only a matter of time, my lad," Sir Francis Wiebe, merchant banker from Halifax town, said, shaking his head and smiling in greeting. "Even cats have only nine lives."

Garrett accepted the outstretched hand with its sausage-like fingers and shook it familiarly, a broad smile creasing his salt-licked features. "Ah, but it's to live those lives, and what a better way to live, eh, kind sir?"

"Go on with your cheek." Sir Francis encased their clasped hands with his other, his natural affection overcoming the fear of the moment now they were all ashore.

"'Tis providence, then, that I made it through yet again." Garrett dropped the gripped hand. "Yet your being here fools no one, Wiebe. 'Tis not concern for my well-being that pulls you from the comfort of bed and a well-rounded arse to warm it. Old miser that you are, you want to make good on your investment."

The older man laughed quietly. The high color in his cheeks blossomed while his palms covered the quaver of his ample stomach. Together, he and Garrett moved out of earshot of the other sailors and walked up the rocky bank, allowing the seamen to start unloading the cargo to the waiting wagons. For such a stout figure, Wiebe climbed without loss of breath.

"You're too much like your father, you young rogue. And besides, who could blame me, my fine fellow?" Wiebe pulled at the lapels of his expensive fur-lined coat. "'Twas relief, true enough, when the messenger arrived to notify me of the signal. You were expected a fortnight ago. I have made one excuse after another for my being in this dreary part of the countryside and not back in my fine house in Halifax."

"An excuse to service your mistress well, you ol' scoundrel, nothing more," Garrett returned, sweeping up a handful of pebbles into his palm and tossing them one by one as he and Wiebe meandered up the hill. "Do not blame me for your extended pleasures."

Wiebe's face puckered, then split in a smile. The

buttonlike eyes crinkled with mirth; the light of mischief twinkled in their depths. "Do not distract me, now. We are on borrowed time, as you well know."

"Ah, but the cargo be worth your wait." Garrett patted the banker on the back.

His father had made this man rich beyond expectation when his own exploits removed a man who called himself Tommy Two-Guns from local power. To continue his endeavors and further the family business, Mackenzie McGuire had sought and found the perfect business liaison in Wiebe, who'd become like a second father to Garrett these last years.

"Better delayed than not at all, when there is so much profit to be had, eh, old friend."

"How you manage it…" Wiebe paused, then turned to watch the progress of the men on the beach.

Like the many cogs in a precision clock, the seamen and laborers worked as an efficient unit. They progressed swiftly, moving the loaded longboats back and forth from ship to shore. "'Tis our good fortune the British are distracted by Napoleon's goings-on, so that a simple merchant like myself can away with a few barrels of our smoothest Scottish whisky and fine French brandy."

"Oh, har." Wiebe snagged his thumbs into the loops of his belt. "What about the Americans?"

"Weather, my old friend. Both friend and foe. The ol' bitch tossed us hither and to, promising we'd join the ghost ships of Sable Island this go round." Garrett gripped Wiebe's shoulder in a quick squeeze. "'Twas only a sound soothing. She relented to allow us passage."

"My word, you speak of the sea as though a living

being."

Garrett turned to the sound of the waves lapping innocently at the beach as though to never bring any harm. He'd grown up with the stories of his parent's adventures at sea and bided his time for his own moment. Now she offered everything he'd been promised.

He lifted his chin and sniffed. "Oh…she is that, my friend," he murmured. "More demanding than any other paramour. A courtesan who demands your very essence, who takes nothing less than everything."

"Well that she left the cargo intact, then. For my luck, you made it." Wiebe began moving back toward the slackening activity. "You'll push down the coast from here," he remarked, already knowing the answer as they exchanged satchels of correspondence, invoices, and payment.

With a tilt to his head, Wiebe jiggled his three chins toward the leather bag. "There be a letter from the old captain himself in there for you."

A warning tingle traveled the length of Garrett's spine. Retaining his cordial mask, he nodded. "We'll leave afore the tide's complete."

They moved to the first of the line of three wagons, inspecting the contents to the barrels of French brandy that would triple Wiebe's investment in a time when quality spirits were scarce. Political unrest always created profitable business.

Done, and Wiebe appeased, Garrett returned to the cliff to scout the lightening horizon. From there, he watched his old friend leave with the bundled cargo, safeguarding his future income.

Garrett returned his attention to the sea. From his

vantage, she appeared as an innocuous mirror wherever his sight scanned. Only those familiar with her workings knew the deep disquiet under the surface. Far below, the sheltered cove hid their very existence, but that granted no guarantee of safety. The stakes seemed to escalate with each trip. The business proved, as Wiebe alluded, to be a certain tightrope he walked with a steady gait as he played each side against the other to achieve his end. Under his father's tutelage, and winning his trust with the family's enterprise, he refused to form allegiances with either side.

With the breaking dawn turning the purple night to a rosy morning, he was ever more cautious as his keen eyes pierced the gloom. This was the most dangerous time of the day. From here he could see far out to sea. Nothing. He relaxed his stance, filled his lungs with the fresh morning air peppered with the scents of the evergreen forest to his back, and prepared to read the correspondence from his father.

"Capt'in." The huffed, slightly high-pitched voice pulled him from his thoughts. Small pebbles cascaded down the steep slope to herald the arrival of the young deck lad, no more than ten or twelve. "Capt'in McGuire, sir, as you see, the last of the wagons has left. Quartermaster's asking permission to grant the men their tot of rum."

Garrett spared the boy a brief glance. The lad appeared positively frightened standing before him with the light of the morning bouncing off the sweat sheen of his skin, brown eyes large in his face. Garrett hadn't been much older than this lad when his father shipped him off to sea to learn to be a man. "Tell Tippen I'll be down shortly. The men may have their tots by shifts, as

I want sentries on board as well as on land until we sail."

"Aye, Capt'in."

His gaze returned to the boy, where he nodded once in dismissal.

The boy smiled, nodded his head, and stumbled back down the hill, seeming grateful to be away.

Garrett settled on a boulder, face to the breeze, and skimmed the correspondence in turn. His fingers paused at his father's letter. His sire's crisp penmanship graced the front of the parchment. Garrett turned the heavy envelope over, where his fingers played across the waxed family crest. Had he ever forgiven his father for giving up the sea when his mother died?

"If I couldn't have both," his father had said before he set Garrett upon his first ship, his own former Spanish berth, the *Navigator*, under the watchful care and guidance of his father's man Burke, who remained to this day his most trusted captain of the fleet, "then I'll have neither."

Garrett watched the lad slither down the face of the hill on his backside. Alone once more, he savored the weight of the document in brief contemplation of what news it might hold before breaking the distinctive family seal of three ships, sails filled with wind, heading to some unknown destination.

With a last glance to the horizon, he turned his gaze to his own three-masted, twelve-gunned brig-sloop. The *Isle Sky* was a strong, fast ship even when loaded down with the best liqueurs he could procure. He heard the general laughter and good-natured banter rise up on the breeze as news spread that the captain gave leave to enjoy a tot. With all that they had gone through on board these last weeks, his men deserved this slight reprieve.

The pending day's brightness raced like a chariot across the pink-hued sky, finally providing Garrett with enough light to read by. Relaxed on his seat, his elbows rested upon his thighs, he set aside his mental list of what needed to be done before they set sail and focused his attention on the letter in hand.

London, 17 March, 1798

Dear Son,

It is with a heavy heart that I must relay the most sad and painful intelligence. Your stepmother, my wife, has died. She had become afflicted with the morbid sore throat shortly after the strong north winds brought the worst of the winter weather inland. Though a doctor was procured most immediately, and she confined to her bed, she succumbed to her fever by the day's break just a fortnight ago.

Garrett rubbed at an imagined kink at the base of his neck, turning his scrutiny to the umbrella sky. He watched as dusty purple clouds skidded across the horizon, pondering the philosophical debate of heaven and hell. Which would the "Lady" Matilda, as she had liked to be referenced, forcefully enter? Her nasal whine would be certain to draw attention from both directions. How very different she'd been from the fiery-haired beauty of his mother.

His father had married too soon in an effort to provide a mother to his young son, and once trapped, found every other occupation to give him solace.

Try as he might, Garrett could muster no great feeling of loss for the woman who had claimed the role of mother these last years. Without doubt, she had

9

proven as much a disappointment to him as she had been to his father in her inability to conceive a back-up heir.

In these last ten years that you have been away, you have provided evidence of a man capable of not only building a successful enterprise from our fleet, despite my misgivings of your methods, but expanding our merchant connections.

His father, now a well-respected merchant, couldn't, given his own history, protest Garrett's seeming lack of loyalty to the Crown. As further evidence, he never refused the accumulated bounty that filled the family's coffers.

Though I know well the pull of the sea, it is now past the time when you must return to your rightful place as my heir…

Despite his advancing years, old Captain Mackenzie McGuire remained ever competitive to further the family fortunes, if not necessarily to wealth, certainly to the prestige of name. Having aligned himself to a title with his second marriage, he wanted the same for his one and only child. Garrett drew breath and wished he too had a tot of rum to quell the tightening of his gut. Here was the letter he had been dreading.

Garrett's hand fisted the corner of the missive, rolling and unrolling the edge as he controlled the sudden urge to set it aflame and pretend he'd never received the correspondence. Marry. As sole heir, his father expected him to return home to wed, produce legitimate sons, and continue the legacy. The matrimonial contract to Beverly MacLeod had been drawn up before his own mother's death birthing a brother who lived only long enough to draw a few short breaths. This legal pact would finally fulfill a longstanding family alliance to bridge the McGuire name to one with a title to accompany and legitimize the wealth.

With their lands sharing a common border, the three MacLeod siblings and he had been tossed together as children, growing up as a school of fish—he and two sisters and an older brother, Brian, who'd become Garrett's lifelong friend. In fact, being of an age with Brian, he and Brian had both taken to the sea the same year, though on different vessels. Now Brian and he served together, Garrett as captain and Brian as his second.

Though he wasn't opposed to the family, marriage to Beverly held no attraction. Garrett shook his head, struggling to continue through the lengthy missive. Despite his best efforts, which in fact, represented little to no enthusiasm, he had no great regard for Beverly. True too, he remained in no doubt of her mutual disregard for him.

He rubbed the roughened stubble on his chin and tried to imagine his betrothed. Bollocks. Though it had been nigh on five years since he had last laid eyes upon her, he could not imagine she was anything more than the spoiled child she had been when he had last known her.

The sun glanced off the mirrorlike surface of the water in a fiery blaze, highlighting the blue and green tones. He lifted his nose and sniffed the air. They would need to set off soon.

In thinking of the MacLeods, he considered the youngest of the clan, Anne. They too had lost a mother to childbirth. While they had seemed to be left to fend for themselves, Beverly assumed the matron's role, while Anne, despite her youth, tried to run wild and convince him and Brian she was equal to a boy and should be allowed to join their games.

"Bessy the Brave" she had coined herself as she strove to keep pace with him and her brother. Garrett traced a thumb along his lip, pinching back the smile as he recalled her scrappy nature. He often wondered, but never asked, how she fared. He closed his eyes and easily remembered a face often soiled, skirts drawn up and tied to allow her the freedom to run until her nanny—or worse still, her sister—would find her out and report back to the household.

Roaming his fingers over the raised ink on the paper, he allowed the small smile to curve his lips. Anne never ran in fright from the scolding, but at the first opportunity, while he and Brian practiced swords or the like, her slight frame would be seen to slip away to the woods surrounding their property.

As a youth, sometimes he would follow. He couldn't help himself, curious to her nature, like one to a wood nymph. There he discovered the young girl, safely away from confines imposed in a rigid house, would come alive with exploration and wonder. How she had intrigued him when he was a young lad.

But he wasn't a young lad any longer. He was a grown man of four and twenty, and he'd been summoned home. At that moment Garrett felt the cuffs of society secure around his wrists, the jailer's whip at his back.

There was no running away from his duty. Straightening his spine to the inevitable, he stood, preparing to return to the beach, cast one last look to the horizon, and froze.

Chapter Two

Anne Elizabeth MacLeod pulled the comb through her sister's fine blonde hair, curled it around her finger, then pinned it into place. Smiling at the result, she couldn't help ruefully comparing her own unruly, too-red locks. Try as she might—and she had to be honest with herself, at least, she didn't take the care her sister did, but when she did—she could never achieve the same smooth, fashionable look.

Repeating the process, she enjoyed the intimacy with her sister. Having affixed multiple pinwheels around the base of Beverly's head, she secured the ribbon and stood back to survey the result.

"Beautiful," she said, fingers steepled under her chin. "It's like your hair wants to do your beauty justice. Yours is certainly the reason Father refers to a woman's hair as her crowning glory."

Her older sister accepted the compliment as intended. Anne breathed easy, forever on alert when she allowed a comment to simply leave her lips without careful deliberation. The avoidance of constant admonishments and the resulting squabbling had caused Anne to spend as much time away from her sister's domain as possible.

Anne didn't blame Beverly for her role in their family. What choice had she been given? Certainly, they hadn't always been that way. Anne did remember when they were fast companions, but when Mama died, their distant father, Gerald MacLeod, left running of house and home to his eldest daughter. This apparently included Anne, although he never asked either for their opinion on the matter.

Father, a distant man by nature, had only just remarried after all these years. For so long, the sisters had only each other. In this, Beverly had made the running of house and home her own, and while she had recently been persuaded to share some with the new woman of the house, she continued, as she had most of Anne's life, in the role of matriarch. Their older brother Brian had turned to the sea when he reached an acceptable age.

To some, Beverly may have appeared overbearing, but Anne knew the difference. Bevvy always placed the interest of Anne first, even when Anne herself did not immediately appreciate the gesture.

Turning, Beverly reached up to lay her palms along Anne's cheeks, which turned hot with the sudden attention. "This is your year, dear sister," Beverly cooed, then stood and kissed her cheek. She returned to the dressing table and handed Anne the cream-colored ribbon, complete with blue cameo, to tie around her neck. Locking eyes through the reflection in the mirror, Beverly continued, "No wallflowers this season, my dear." She nodded with significance, her eyes bright. "We all agreed. Father assured me of only the best balls for his daughters."

"Now that he has a new wife, he wants only to be rid of us. And as you are already spoken for, he no longer wants me underfoot." Anne looped the bow with flourish. "He's positively changed. Brian won't

15

recognize him when he comes home next. If he comes home—"

"Shush now, dear sister." Beverly turned to grip Anne's shoulders. "If only you were a little more, as you say, underfoot. How long did it take me to wrangle you to the dressing room today?" She flapped her fingers and shook her head. "That is contrary to the discussion. The reasons for Father's favor do not matter. Not at all. All that matters is finding the right match."

Anne smiled indulgently at her sister's vivacious face. Unlike Anne, Bevvy's cheeks did not blotch with color when excited. Instead, the cream of her complexion became suffused by a pastel pink like the bloom on a petal fresh with morning dew.

She lowered her gaze to peer at the tips of her new silk shoes, currently pinching her toes. Much as Anne tried, she could live three lifetimes and never be the honey that attracted popularity like her sister. She didn't like the dressing up and parading around to be sorted and judged. In this, she yearned for her brother's practical ways, missing him terribly. In Brian's company she never had to practice to please. Why could she not have been born with the freedom to roam, be who she was without fear of scolding?

Resigned, she raised her gaze to meet her sister's. She felt the pull of Bevvy the same as everyone else who ever met her. Could the attraction stem from the fact that Beverly did not seek a match, having been betrothed almost since infancy? Is this why she could fan and flatter, always the most sought after in any occasion? Could this be the source of freedom Anne longed for?

Anne spoke of this contemplation. "That is all well and fine, dear Bevvy. You are already matched."

Beverly rolled her eyes heavenward. "For all that I ever see or have seen my betrothed." She turned to pat her hair lightly, then swooped to retrieve her wrap. "How do you seem to know so much? You've been more attentive than I suspected. But I do wonder if there is an actual match, since I've no real proof of his existence."

Anne shrugged, composing her features into a mask of nonchalance. Defiant as always, her heart thumped at the thought of Garrett McGuire. In all likelihood, the son of their neighbor, companion of her brother, and fiancé to her sister, would have no recollection of the child she'd been when last they met.

By turn, Garrett McGuire would have no cause to warrant Anne's existence any measure with Beverly long since promised through their families' ancient connection. Try as she might to forget him, he crept into Anne's dreams when she least expected. These were the times she longed never to wake. For only in her dreams would she be the one in the white veil. Guilt consumed her whenever this occurred. She'd wake with a cold sweat and misery over her heart at the betrayal of her sister.

How could she profess to love her sister, when she longed for the husband?

"'Tis a long road from promise to reality, dear sister," Beverly said, pulling her gloves up the length of her arm, seemingly unaware of the turbulent emotions raging within Anne. "Until he presents himself, I shall not put my stock in the legitimacy."

Anne felt her eyes widen. As ever, she could not

17

fathom her sister's disregard for the one Anne so longed for most. How torn were her affections! Could it be true that Bevvy preferred another? How had she not noticed? Wasn't Henry Rathmore also betrothed?

"Bevvy, you mustn't say such things."

"Oh, Annie, my love." Bevvy's laughter rang like music around the chamber. Her fingers pinched her cheeks, drawing more bloom. "Do not concern yourself. I am, as you say, already spoken for. We must concentrate on you."

Anne blinked rapidly. "But I find these balls so dreadfully boring." She raised the hem of the underskirt to reveal her silken three-inch-heeled slipper. "Unlike you, I'm not made for these things. I stumble over my own feet in these outrageous heels."

Even without slippers, Beverly towered over Anne's five-foot frame. "Do not fret, my lovely one. You are proportionate and lovely in all ways that matter. It's the fact that you don't make yourself heard that is the problem. This shyness and preoccupation with books leads you away from the enjoyment."

"And heels will make me be heard?" Anne pulled a face in the mirror. "You and Father's new bride, Harriet, have told me often enough men don't like opinionated women. Was this a falsehood?"

"No, no, my dear." Beverly pulled her top lip between her teeth. She tipped her head to the side, released her lip, and puffed out her cheeks. "In this one thing at least, our new mother and I are agreed. Participate instead of scowling. I declare, everything you think can be read on your face."

Anne reached to cover her cheeks, praying that was not the case or else her split affections would doom her.

Beverly continued her fussing and talking without notice. "Instead, pretend you are with the old herbalist where you are constantly occupied, and keep those vast vile opinions on politics to yourself when men are present. Actually, dear sister, keep them to yourself in front of the majority of our acquaintances."

Her sister paused, stepped back, and scrutinized her from head to toe. The straight straw-blonde brows drew together in contemplation. Then she lifted a delicate finger to her lips, scrutinized the digit, and took Anne's hands away from her face to cradle them in her own, presenting a pair of gloves which matched her dress. "And be sure not to remove your gloves. Those green stains are not attractive."

Anne pulled one of her ungloved hands free of the embrace. She'd scrubbed for what seemed like hours, but still the tips had retained a slight green hue.

"And...no frowning." Beverly's periwinkle-blue eyes crinkled at the corners. "There, I've gone and made such a shambles. I was supposed to encourage." She smiled and pulled Anne close, enfolding her in a warm embrace. "Forget about that just now. The heels. We were discussing your slippers. They will allow you to be seen, and the men will then lean in to hear you and request your hand for a dance."

"Really?" Anne questioned skeptically, removing the silk slipper for inspection. "All that from one pair of shoes?"

Her sister took an indulgent breath. "Oh, bother." She grinned back at Anne's reflection. "Men can't notice what they can't see. The heels will ensure you don't look like a small child. I will not allow you to sit by yourself. Hence, you will dance and enjoy yourself."

19

"Just like that." Anne giggled. "You make it sound so easy."

"And it is." Beverly took Anne's hand and started for the bed where Anne's shawl lay ready to be draped over her small frame. "You and I will stay close together, and you will be well cared for."

Anne inspected herself in the gilded mirror. Old Gavin Dun from the village, who taught her about medicines, called her scrawny but, with her hair color, bright as a firefly. Harriet categorized her as slight, telling her it made her appear much younger than her eighteen years.

Anne pulled a face, stuck her fingers in her ears, and stuck out her tongue. "All any of you ever think about is matchmaking."

Beverly swiped Anne's hands down to her sides. "Is there anything else?" Bevvy tittered.

Anne could think of plenty, but held her opinion. Two years older, Beverly took after their mother with her fair hair and height that placed her perfectly level with most men's shoulders. From this vantage point she could easily display her gifted ability of creating conversation from thin air. Whereas everything Anne ever found interesting—such as medicine and literature—was frowned upon in polite society.

"The usual partners will be there, so no need for concern. I am sure dear Henry Rathmore will be in attendance and take pity as usual."

Was that a confirmation of Bevvy's true interest? "Dear Henry, is it?" Anne quipped back.

Bevvy flapped her gloved fingers. But her eyes took on a glitter Anne hadn't noticed before. "Yes, he's always such a gentleman to ask me to dance when no other would dare, knowing I am promised elsewhere."

Anne knew this to be a blatant lie, but one said in jest. Beverly normally had little opportunity to catch her breath between dances.

"Don't make a fuss. I told you, tonight is for you. Father tells me he has a most special introduction to make."

"For me?"

Bevvy bit her lip. "Not that he was specific, but I understood his meaning to be for you, as he appeared most concerned that you be properly attired for the evening."

"Oh?" Anne was interested despite herself, and all the hair on her arms rose. This would be a first for their father. Perhaps marriage had altered his mental state more than she imagined. He was little enough involved in their lives, but since his marriage to the Lady Harriet seemed keen on their social acceptance. For him to not only express an interest but be present at the ball to make an introduction was monumental. "No changing into my plain muslin, then."

Beverly's face looked horror struck with the very idea. "Certainly not. The silk. Always the silk."

Anne didn't suppress a giggle and laid her palm on top of her sister's and squeezed encouragingly. "Then lead on, my dear."

Chapter Three

The ball offered little to distract and more to disappoint than Anne had feared. Worse, as she wobbled on the heels, trying not to sprain an ankle, her feet ached, contributing to her overall misery. Despite an elaborate up-do, one frizzy orange lock continued to feather across her eyes, creating an added irritation. Every time she flicked it away, she found herself scolded for fidgeting.

Shortly after the formal introductions to their hosts, Bevvy had kept a close hand on her arm as the two circled around the dancers, and she provided instructions and support. Then, as always happened, without fault of her sister, Bevvy was whisked away to admire one thing or another, like all popular people.

Upon her return, she pointed her fan breathlessly. "There is Walter Willard, son of a baron. He would make a handsome husband."

Anne jerked at Bevvy's sudden appearance, and her neck creaked. Beverly took no notice as she spoke close to her ear. "I have come to rescue you." Anne's gratitude almost overwhelmed her. She'd felt so alone and at a loss as to how to partake or mingle within existing circles of conversation.

"Ah, my dear sister," Bevvy said, hand across her mouth to conceal a smile. "You are as jumpy as a rabbit. We must really get you on the dance floor to

22

exhaust that nervous energy. Where is your card?"

"Who's nervous? Anne? Nonsense. What's to be nervous about?"

Their stepmother had joined them. Harriet seemed unable to modulate her tone. Her voice seemed always too high to Anne and always drew unwelcomed attention. Holding a handkerchief to her nose, she sniffed and stepped to Anne's other side. "I see your gaze directed to Arthur Willard's youngest."

Anne hadn't noticed one over the other, being so concerned about keeping out of anyone's immediate attention. With Harriet's words, she focused on the young man with a wobbly face and prominent front teeth. The sparse mustache did little to improve the overall picture.

Harriet lowered the cloth, refolded it, then sniffed. Her nose wrinkled, and she shook her head. "Move on." Her voice held a note of command, and she pivoted so her shoulder now blocked the view of the young man. "Being the heir's spare, he's therefore penniless. Onward to better prospects."

Bevvy tittered and shook her head. She tugged on Anne's sleeve and maneuvered her from her rooted position toward the dining room. Leaving their stepmother behind, Bevvy pointed out one eligible bachelor after another. If looks were to be considered, the wait staff held better options. If she were seeking intelligence, surely none present would be eligible, as they would be wise to stay at home. Still, the conversation centered on annual income, homes, family connections, and access.

Bevvy lowered her head close to Anne's ear and whispered, "Oh, Annie, my dear, I tell you I am on pins and needles."

The hand on Anne's arm held a slight tremor, and Anne became alert.

"Why? For what?"

"Oh, you." Beverly brushed her fingers along Anne's arm. "Why, to be married, of course. It seems I have been engaged most of my life. I am ready to be wife. Perhaps mother."

Picturing Bevvy weighted down by pregnancy scorched Anne with an instant terror at memory of the loss of their own mother while attempting to deliver another son to their father. She and Garrett had that in common—the loss of their mothers to childbirth. A shiver of pleasure and pain brought the hair on her arms erect, thinking of her sister's future husband. Her cheeks flamed to betray her guilt and shame to even ponder the memory of a childhood acquaintance always destined to be her brother through marriage.

"What's wrong, dearest?" Beverly asked. "Your color's higher than normal. My goodness, you're redder than your hair. Who has caused this reaction? I must know at once. You sly creature, you do have your eye set on someone."

Anne laid trembling fingers on her sister's elbow. "The thought of you settled, dear Bevvy, makes me both happy and sad, for then we would be truly separated."

"Nonsense." Bevvy gripped Anne's arm, and her eyes shone. "Never, my dear. Whoever shall be husband to me will be brother to you. We will be as we were as children when we play with our own kids."

Anne had few memories of Beverly actually playing. More times than not, she performed the

24

matronly duty of constant discipline.

"Of course, you would always be welcome," she continued. "We will never be but a few miles apart, after all."

Anne pursed her lips and rubbed a pinkie above her brow. Were they speaking of the ever-absent Garrett McGuire? Her definite suspicions that Beverly had contravening plans to that of their father seemed to grow. Surely Bevvy would never go against what had been arranged for so long.

"But Garrett is a sailor. A captain now, I hear. Like our Brian, he spends so much time across the water in the Americas. What would happen if he intends for you to settle there?"

Beverly's eyes widened, and very unnaturally, her face drained of color from bad to worse. "Garrett." The normal peach complexion disappeared, and her face fell.

Further discussion halted when all at once Anne found herself standing before Henry Rathmore. He perfumed the air with the scent of applewood and sour body. Likely the aroma was more pronounced to her due to her proximity. Her nose came almost level with his underarm. Taking a step back, she wrinkled her nose and turned her head slightly away.

Anne need not have concerned herself with the movement being noticed. Other than to spare her a glare, which traveled the length of his Roman beak of a nose, he turned his fancy to her sister. His squared face split almost by half in a broad grin, making his eyes crinkle.

"Good lady Beverly, may I reserve the next dance?"

Bevvy's glowing complexion returned. Her gaze dipped, and her chin followed in a demure response, while her lashes fluttered. Anne felt certain all previous concerns were forgotten.

"You do me great honor, Mister Rathmore," she said. Then linking her arm through Anne's, she drew her close. "You remember my dear sister, Anne?"

"Indeed," he responded. His gaze returned to Anne. "Though your sister has mentioned you, I have not had the pleasure."

Anne looked upon him with new eyes. She'd seen Rathmore often but knew without doubt he took no notice of anyone aside from her sister.

His stiff bow acknowledged Anne before his eagle-like nose repositioned to again focus his gaze on Beverly. The tip of his tongue appeared to lick his lips, giving Anne every impression her sister provided his next quarry. Then the music paused, and he held out his arm. "May I?"

Beverly smiled adoringly and laid her slender, gloved hand lightly on his bent elbow. She turned her head back toward Anne. "I will find you directly after," Bevvy said before stepping closer to Rathmore. "We will find you the perfect partner for the next set."

That her sister didn't imagine they would meet on the dance floor did not concern Anne. She had little to persuade her that she missed anything by assuming the sidelines. In fact, the observation of others had become a prized game to guess and imagine who next would partner. Her reluctance did not stem from inability. In fact, through Beverly's tutelage, she was quite practiced at the steps. Still, she remained wary of the crowd, happier not to be required to create idle chat.

Anne pasted a smile upon her lips, though her feet ached to be out of the terrible slippers. The additional height made her feel awkward and foreign, as though she would tumble over at any moment. Continuing to circle the assembly, she drew ever closer to the gilded tapestry which hung on the wall. Failing a hole in the floor, perhaps she would find a door behind the rug and make her escape. The press of people filled her with an urgent desire to be outside where the air was still crisp with spring newness.

Yes, she decided, she'd form some excuse to give her father and sister. Leave a message with Harriet. Besides, she'd been more of a burden and they'd be glad she'd gone. Of a sudden, her mind danced with the thought of an evening where she could study her herbal books without interruption of criticism on wasting her time.

Convinced she'd get away with her plan, Anne cast a backward glance to the ballroom and reached for the edge of the curtain. In such a hurry and not paying attention, she walked right out of her slipper. This caused her to trip directly into the broad back of a tall man suddenly in her way. Catching her breath in a gasp, she stumbled back. Looking around, she spotted her slipper. Rather than bend, she tried to retrieve her shoe with her toe, all the while praying her faux pas would go unnoticed.

Then the man turned.

A calm brown gaze settled upon her, and she found she was winded. Heat flared, and the already warm atmosphere sizzled. Breath neither entered nor left. The room became a vacuum, and her mouth gaped open in shock—Garrett McGuire.

The eyes which gazed upon her crinkled at the edge, revealing a mesh of lines not present years before. Sun-bronzed skin gave evidence of a life outside. As his smile spread, the familiarity of the expression allowed her breath to return. The full lower lip begged her attention. She bit her own lip in response.

His gaze drifted around her face, down her frame, and back to her lips before re-focusing. Her nerves tingled as though he physically touched her.

"This is a most interesting way to be reacquainted," he said, humor evident in his deep tones. The manly voice bore only echoes from the youth she remembered.

One hand wrapped around his glass, the other swung to push his jacket flap back to settle on his hip. He had such command, such presence, Anne could only stare.

"You may have tugged on my sleeve. There's no need to slam into me." He paused to lift his drink. "Had this been full, I would have surely spread its contents over all who surrounded."

She blinked several times, aware of both his and his companion's eyes now upon her. "Garrett," Anne finally muttered, trying to keep the shock from her voice. "Ah, I mean Mister McGuire. You have returned."

In a slow deliberate arc, his hand came forward and brushed at the annoying lock of hair and settled the piece behind her ear as easily as if he'd been doing such a gesture their whole lives. "There's no need for titles between friends, is there, my Bessy?"

The use of the aged pet name further flamed her cheeks with, she was sure, the beastly splotches of color. Where was her escape? Her fists clenched and unclenched as she struggled to remember any social norm acceptable in such a situation. She was confounded on how to respond to the unexpected familiarity.

In order to leave, she must first retrieve her shoe. Bevvy would never forgive her if she ran off barefooted.

Beneath the camouflage of her voluminous skirts, Anne's toe continued to seek the fugitive slipper. Balanced on one foot, she tried to stand tall to impress Garrett with her extension. With an effort, she curtsied awkwardly on one leg. "I am Miss Anne, Mister McGuire. A child no longer, sir, at almost eighteen."

"I stand corrected, Miss Anne." He smiled down at her, the brown eyes velvet with merriment, and she no longer craved an escape from, but rather an escape with this all-too-familiar man. "Though you will forgive me if I continue to insist on plain Garrett between friends."

"I see you have reacquainted yourself with my younger daughter, McGuire." Her father brushed past to shake hands with Garrett. "You have arrived as promised by that old scoundrel of a father of yours. I had hoped you would, and I feel it will be a wonderous surprise to our Beverly."

With those words, spoken as only her father could, Anne hobbled to the side to allow the men to pass in their conversation.

Garrett strode only a few paces though, when he paused to turn and look her way. Immediately she cast her gaze to the floor so as not to be caught staring, for she knew all of her feelings would be revealed upon her face. Bevvy had so often told her she was an open book, and she felt sure she could hide nothing from this man.

Her stomach turned over while her heart announced a double tempo. Yet she had to concede—her childhood crush on a boy she once knew must end here and now. She would never hurt Bevvy with her foolish fancy.

As her toes reached and fumbled for her elusive slipper, shame burned again. Anne prayed for some catastrophic event that would cause the floor to swallow her whole. The small flame that had begun to dance again upon seeing Garrett flickered and died, as it must. The room pressed in against her, the sounds too loud, the smells overpowering in their extravagance. She must be away. Sidling sideways in vain, she tried to slip her shoe over her foot without aid.

Foul words of frustration raged in her mind, all the wonderful vulgarity she'd often heard in the stables when no one knew she was about. Oh, to be a man and not have to worry about such propriety.

Standing within a pace of the ballroom entrance in conversation with her father, Garrett flickered his amused gaze back to her. In horror of being found out, she watched his brows draw together over the bridge of his straight nose in question as he slid his eyes down the length of her gown to the floor. As she watched, unable to look away, he turned to murmur something to her father and set his glass down. As though it were the most natural thing in the world, he closed the distance between them, bent, retrieved her slipper, reached under her skirt for her foot, and slid the shoe over her stocking. Retaining hold of her foot, he glanced up at her face and gave her a wink before patting her ankle.

Without an utterance, he stood, rejoined her father,

and resumed his conversation with the man, who appeared to notice nothing untoward. Yet her leg tingled with warmth where his hand had cupped her ankle.

"'Tis never to be. Not now. Not ever," she whispered.

The open door leading to the garden beckoned just ahead. Needing no further inducement, Anne raced through the barrier and into the shelter of newly budded flowers.

Chapter Four

In the hum of the room after coming face to face with the one person he wasn't yet ready to meet, Garrett strove to concentrate on the old man's conversation. Though he knew he couldn't avoid the sister of his bride-to-be for long, somehow his memory of Anne did not correlate with her presence at a ball.

While Gerald nattered on about the fine qualities of his eldest daughter, Garrett found his only interest lay in the display of how the man's bushy mustache ruffled and bounced with the tempo of his banter. He seemed rather changed in his newly married state. Some people were like that, once married they felt everyone should partake. At last, Gerald ran out of compliments regarding Beverly's virtues and, with what struck Garrett as relief, and a deep sigh, moved on to politics.

Unable to resist, Garrett cast a quick glance over his shoulder. Anne was nowhere to be seen. Still, the startled wide, green eyes occupied his thoughts, burned fresh into the images he'd harbored of her for years, leaving him little to contribute to the exchange.

During the long voyage he'd resigned himself, or thought he had, to the circumstance. Per his mother's wish and his father's insistence, he'd be married and unite two families long intertwined. In the end, he concluded, he would proceed under his own terms. He'd abide by the contract, but marriage did not—

would not—bind him to the land. He and Beverly had no great emotional connection. Once he managed an heir, he would continue to build the McGuire empire through shipping, perhaps even purchase land abroad. He'd found a lovely parcel in New Scotland which would offer a fresh start away from the stuffy and tired traditions he'd come to abhor. There was little left to be conquered or explored on this island empire awash in dandies, and like his sire, he craved the excitement and adventure of actually living.

Garrett took his time to stroll down the hall, greeting old acquaintances as he went, until he reached the ballroom. There, he watched Beverly circle the floor with Rathmore. Fortunately, she had yet to notice him. Perhaps she hadn't been told to expect him. As he leaned a shoulder against the wall, crossing one booted foot over the other, he wondered if she even remembered what he looked like or would recognize him if she did. They'd been but children the last time they spoke. At the time, a fresh youth himself, looking forward to any excuse for an escapade, he spared little attention for the opposite sex. He recalled how, as he had run to the woods with her brother, Brian, she called after him, quite haughtily, that one day he would be her husband and forced to regard her opinion.

"Puh," he said, echoing the same sentiments of his youth.

On the rare occasions he had thought of Beverly in the intervening years, it was regarding that strange point of wondering how she had reached that conclusion. Their union would always be a matter of arrangement, never a bond as his parents' had been, of love and devotion. Though previously uncertain what

33

he would find back on home soil, he saw little to no motivation to change the life he currently led, regardless of having a wife.

Enjoying the claret, he sipped the wine and took the opportunity to observe his betrothed. Blonde curls swung, her head swaying from side to side, as she maneuvered beautifully around the ballroom in the arms of another. Garrett could admit the lady had character. She'd been bred to be a hostess. Clearly the coquet tilt of her face, an offered cheek, and demure eyes had Rathmore enthralled. The sheen of her smooth skin, combined with the double complement of the honey curls and blue eyes, which danced merrily even at the distance of the dance floor, would be enough to hold any man.

Yet he felt unmoved. Not a stirring. He tried to imagine her in his arms and felt no attraction. Conversely, his palm held a whisper of a tingle where he'd held a tiny foot which trembled as he replaced the lost slipper. Strange but not unexpected considering their kinship as children despite the age difference. He couldn't suppress a wry grin, for the disparity in maturity seemed little now.

On impulse, he searched the floor for the tiny, awkward, bright-headed Anne. He remembered a girl with a throaty laugh and eyes the color of moss. Earthy, warm, comfortable. His hands gripped, then released with the memory of her soft skin. This ballroom with all its formality was not an environment meant for his Bessy.

His Bessy?

No. Not his. She had corrected him. A girl no longer, she'd said. Anne.

34

No. Bessy.

Garrett ran a thumb and forefinger across his freshly shaved chin. He must not allow his thoughts of Anne to gain traction. There on the dance floor, comfortable, it seemed, in the arms of another, glided what was to be his bride. He'd reconciled to this. He'd had the entire voyage to prepare. Their families had expectations. Their peers equally so. He'd told himself a boyhood fancy could not last.

He wished he could say he'd thought little of his Bessy, these years away. But he would not lie to himself. War of expectation had constantly waged as he strove to escape the decisions made for him without ever having included him.

"Damn it," he muttered.

"Pardon?"

Garrett coughed and lowered his hand back to his waist. He raised his glass to Gerald, who'd come up beside him. "Empty so quickly, and no one about to provide a refill."

"They will be around shortly."

"I'm sure," he returned. "However, if you'll excuse me, I will seek out the cellar stock from its source."

"Surely not before saying hello to Beverly," her father said, sweeping an arm to the couples on the floor. "It will conclude shortly."

Garrett smiled and laid a hand on the man's shoulder. "'Tis a long night yet, Gerald, and plenty of time." He molded his lips in an indulgent smile. "Rathmore provides good company, and I need not disturb since she is not yet expecting me. I will gather refreshments and return to celebrate."

"Oh, yes, there's a good man," Gerald said, his

face lighting with what Garrett concluded was relief. "Well done, McGuire. But do not dally. We wouldn't want to encourage Rathmore's fancy."

Garrett narrowed his gaze in the dancer's direction. Rathmore a rival? Was that a possibility? He shook his head and removed his grip from Gerald. Unlikely. He didn't believe in luck, and this union with Beverly MacLeod had been ordained for too long for a mere fancy to release him from the confines of the contract.

Setting his glass down on a random table, Garrett strode through the crowd toward the refreshments to make his escape. Whisky, direct from the keg, would surely stiffen his resolve. Still, he searched the throngs of assembled people, colorfully arrayed like prancing peacocks, for Anne.

Neither of them belonged at such a place. As much as he was at home on the ocean, she also did not belong in such splendor. He did not imagine she had changed all that much. Unlike her sister, his Bessy belonged to the trees, in the woods. Had she been a man, he could easily have seen her on board a ship, at ease like her brother.

No, she would not be on the ballroom floor smiling coquettishly to a dandy in fine linens. If he wanted to see her, he must look for her where she could feel most comfortable. But did he want to see her?

Yes.

Should he seek her out?

No.

And what would be the purpose of his pursuit? Here he stopped mid stride and braced a hand against the wall. To meet as old friends. To achieve an update on her life, and that of her sister. He likely knew more of her brother than she, and so there might be the basis of conversation. An opportunity. He could regale her with the adventures he and Brian shared.

He slapped his palm to his forehead, slid it over his face to cover his mouth. "By Christ, man, you delude yourself."

Yet, after the marriage to Beverly, Anne would be his sister, so he would have to become used to seeing her in this manner. He would be required to make small conversations. Better to practice. And with this last thought to anchor him, he whirled on the spot and strode to the garden.

Chapter Five

The evil slippers dangled from the tips of Anne's fingers. She'd throw them away if she could imagine a way of getting away with it. She rubbed her thumb along the smooth exterior and decided the scolding wasn't worth the momentary glee of rebellion.

The sweet smells and earthy tang from the garden drew her away from the lights and frolic. Her toes curled into the sponge of grass between the stepping stones, and she began to relax. Here was her comfort. Uncaring that the hem of her fine gown trailed along the garden path, she wandered between the shrubs. The sweet perfume of lilac and rose revived her. She lifted her skirt and stepped over the rock border, leaving the path. The spongy grass and turned soil were much kinder to the pads of her feet.

The dewy air cooled the flame from her cheeks. In the breeze, the annoying lock of hair again fluttered across her eyes. Perhaps if she'd been more to the strawberry blonde instead of the red, she'd be more attractive to potential suiters. But was that what she really wanted? This only served to remind her of Garrett's easy touch in moving it behind her ear. Clearly, he still regarded her like a brother or a parent to a child. Someone in need of looking after in social atmospheres. She stamped her foot. Would that be all she ever was to anyone, a child? Someone to be directed, looked after, a constant burden?

Still holding the strand of coppery hair between her fingers, she yanked the end, which reflected like a penny in the dim light from the mansion. Anne didn't mind the pain from the tug. In fact, she relished the distraction, wanting in that moment to pull all the fuzzing wisps from her scalp.

Annoyed, she swept the tendrils out of the way and, in a gust of wind, more came loose.

"Oh!" She dropped the shoes to the side and rifled her fingers through the ornate up-do, causing the pins to come loose. Soon the locks floated around her shoulders and the pins showered to the ground. As this was her more natural state, she knew she now resembled the fabled medusa, with her curls standing out like the serpents, surrounding her head.

Both Harriet and Bevvy would be ashamed. Perhaps on a brighter note, she need not attend future balls, for her behavior couldn't be trusted.

She dropped to her knees, knowing there would be no escaping these social functions and she was weary of having to be told. Feeling along the ground, she worked to retrieve the pins, although her ability to remake the style was obscure, at best. Pins in hand, she stood and pulled her hair back from her face, twisted the ends up, imagining how she had looked in the mirror. At the time, she had felt she was looking at a different person. Bevvy had done such a wonderful job. Anne's lower lip wobbled. How horrible to destroy what her sister had worked so hard to create.

With effort, she held back her tears and bit her lip to cease the tremor. Knowing she looked a mess, disgraced and disgusted that she'd let her temper get the better of her, she determined not to further impinge on Bevvy's night. The result of her actions meant she had no choice but to avoid the ball for the remainder of the night. This offered little relief to her embarrassment. She dropped back on her haunches, considering her current dilemma. How could Anne make a credible excuse to both her sister and father, never mind Harriet…and how would she meet them without causing a fuss at the end of the evening.

"Bother," she groaned. She leaned over so her forehead connected with the ground. Temper rising again, she banged her fist. The soft side of her palm connected with a sharp object, likely a rock or garden stone, and she felt the skin tear. She couldn't contain the yelp and hopped up, twisting her hand for a better look. She could see hardly anything in the dark, but a warm trickle of blood oozed down her arm. She stepped back, holding her hand at a distance, lost her balance, bumped into the nearby tree, and slid to the ground. Could the evening get any worse?

Giving up, she ripped a small piece of fabric from her petticoat and wrapped her hand, cradling it against her chest. She pulled her knees close, wrapped her good arm around them, and buried her head in the hollow. Just how long would she have to wait before she could leave?

****

Forefinger and thumb pinched his lips while Garrett considered what to do. When she yelped, he started directly off the path toward her, but just prior to announcing himself, something in her manner stopped him. Now he stood under a nearby tree, and as he watched her sit, head bowed, looking entirely defeated, he wondered if he might cause her further distress if he revealed himself.

He had left the ball, if he were honest, in search of Anne. Really, she'd always be his Bessy, and he couldn't wrap his head around the notion of calling her anything else. He intended to tell her as much, but when he couldn't see her, indecision made him pause on the foot path, considering whether to return or simply leave the ghastly event. Poised to return, a movement to the left had drawn his attention. Soon he bore witness to the antics of his Bessy.

The meager glow of the moon seemed to highlight her movements while shadowing his presence. The longer he stood, the more indecisive he became. He likely should have stated his presence, but confirmation she was indeed still the feisty girl he remembered, combined with what he'd witnessed, made him hold his tongue.

Even through the obvious aggravation of loosened hair so she looked like a wild woodland nymph, to the pounding fists and stomping feet, to when she fell back, there was an undeniable grace. Like that of an ancient faerie caught out of her realm. Now as she settled next to the trunk of a large oak, he wanted nothing more than to kiss her palm and then transport her back where she belonged.

The moment stretched and quiet resumed. An occasional bird sang in the distance, and soon the melodies of the ball drifted like the background to a stage production. Seemingly stirred by the clear notes of the waltz, Bessy lifted her face to the moon, giving her an ethereal glow which momentarily paused his heart.

41

Why torture himself? He ran his hand through his hair, then loosened his cravat.

Stepping lightly away, he wandered farther into the dense design of the growth where the vines twined over the path, forming an archway. Here he could no longer see his Bessy, and he determined the same would be true for an accidental sighting of him. He had a sudden urge to preserve her privacy. He didn't want to cause her shame knowing she'd been seen in an instant of awkwardness.

The cuff of his hand scratched against the new stubble on his cheek. Then a tingle of soft giggles perked his attention.

Bessy?

Surely she could not have planned a clandestine meeting? Not her. Not by the state of the rage he'd witnessed.

No, he confirmed, she hadn't moved.

Soon a corresponding distinctly male laugh followed. Breathy sounds of a couple in the midst of a tryst floated with the soft breeze. Garrett turned his head, drawn to the sound. Apparently, he and Bessy were not the only guests drawn to the shadows and privacy of the elaborate garden.

A sailor for many years, Garrett's night vision and hearing were always attuned to even the slightest variation. A certain creak of the deck, the snap of the canvas, the whine of the wind could in equal measures herald danger or fair weather, even proximity to a coast. He was discovering the same on land. The sounds caused the hair on his neck to rise.

These sounds brought to mind a rendezvous of secrecy. The tones of the murmurs a cajoling of sorts.

Someone trying to placate the other and at the same time convince them of something different. Sometimes, he had learned when speaking to the natives of the new world, he didn't need to identify the words to understand meaning in inflection. Communication was a matter of feeling on many levels. This had the markers of a man doing his best to rid the woman of her modesty.

Poised on the balls of his feet, he contemplated whether to continue down the path or retreat to the ball and leave the couple to their privacy and anonymity. Going forward would surely bring him level with the couple, but a withdrawal would alert his Bessy to his proximity. Either left him on the incorrect footing for a man recently returned after being away for years. No, this was no choice at all.

Then the crunch of stone under foot removed his decision. Shadows approached. With little alternative, Garrett reached in his pocket to retrieve a cheroot. Minding the timing, he flamed the match.

As expected, the couple stopped in their tracks. Hands previously clasped now dropped, and the woman lengthened the distance between her and her companion.

An audibly sharp intake of breath. "Garrett?" The question was uttered in a gasp.

He blew out the blueish smoke into the slight breeze. "Miss Beverly," he cooed in his most deliberate of drawls to disguise his own shock. Garrett nodded, then altered his gaze to the man. "Rathmore."

Chapter Six

Anne remained where she was, scared and humiliated by the potential exposure in her current state. Her heart hadn't been able to resume a normal tempo since being alerted that both Garrett and Beverly were in the garden too. In her state, she'd forgotten that Bevvy likely didn't even know Garrett was back in the country and in attendance at the ball. Her sister had assumed the surprise promised by their father had everything to do with Anne and Anne's future. Though she should have known better, Beverly's enthusiasm had been contagious, and Anne had thought the same.

Now, Anne could only hope the couple's reunion would mask Anne's disarray and allow her time and opportunity to slip unnoticed into the carriage. Still, she remained where she hid as she considered. The overall event cast Anne into a state of perplexity. Rathmore? Had no one noticed Bevvy being in the garden—alone—with Henry Rathmore? Why would her sister engage in such frivolous behavior? People would whisper and now, surely, Garrett had noticed them.

Anne's stomach gave a lurch and felt the sudden need to vomit with concern. What would Garrett think? Perhaps, if Anne intervened, she'd take the spotlight off Beverly and Henry's tête-à-tête by moonlight.

Rising to her knees, she shuffled to where she could peer around the tree. The moon had risen, casting a silvery glow between the shadows of the foliage. Garrett's strong back faced her, with a slight side profile of his strong-boned face. On the other side of the walk, she could just make out the edge of Bevvy's pale cheek and the top of Henry's head beyond.

Garrett had a hand in his waistcoat pocket while he drew upon a cheroot. The smoke perfumed the air, adding spice to the sweetness of the garden scents. This subtle smoking, however, didn't fool her. She was not blind to the tense line of his back, or the clench of jaw muscles. She'd known him since childhood and some things never changed, no matter how bland a mask the face presented.

It seemed her whole life she had watched this man from afar. His close relationship with her brother made Anne feel she understood Garrett as well as Brian, from all the time she'd spent following them and trying to partake in their escapades.

She'd always been thwarted and sent away, though. That had only made her more stealthy. She smiled a bit. Either that or they simply gave up chasing her off.

Biting the skin around her thumbnail, Anne wondered if Garrett had actually trailed her sister and paramour into the garden. Conscious of the rustle of her skirt, hoping it would be muted by the strains of the music from within, she adjusted her position for a better view of their faces. If Garrett had followed, she dared not wonder to what end. Did he mean to call Rathmore out? Her nerves stretched at the ramifications.

"Damnation," she muttered and stood, shaking her skirt and hair as she moved from her hiding spot. Stepping back onto the paving stones, she bent to place her shoes on her feet, then stood and gazed at each in turn.

All eyes riveted on Anne, and Bevvy covered her open mouth with a gloved hand.

"Anne," she whispered.

Anne prayed her ankles wouldn't wobble as she looped her arm through her sister's. Mustering courage she didn't feel, she turned to Henry and nodded. Then, as though they hadn't previously met, she focused her gaze on Garrett. "Nice to see you returned to us in one piece."

She led Beverly back through the garden and up the stairs. Whatever the cause of all of them being in various locations of the shrubbery was left for each of them to wonder as she guided her sister through one of the side entrances.

****

Anne made a show of removing the few remaining pins and combed her fingers through her hair as though having it loose at a ball was expected. Beverly didn't take the time to scold. She was completely absorbed in her own considerations.

Her gloved hands patted her cheeks. "Just when I had given up," Bevvy whispered in the carriage on the way home. She lowered her hands to her lap. "Though he is certainly more dashing than I recalled, he is still no Henry Rathmore."

Anne's gaze flew to their father, who stared brooding out the window. Harriet dozed on his shoulder. With each bump, their father's new wife snorted awake, opened her eyes briefly, and settled back, seemingly unaware of or unconcerned about what had transpired at the ball.

Anne remained rigid in her seat. She felt her brows

rise and her eyes widen at the comment. How her sister could book any comparison between Garrett McGuire and Henry Rathmore eluded her. One may as well compare the luster of the moon to the inside of a cave. The two could not be linked.

Then her sister said something which caused Anne's heart to stop altogether. "What?" she said, louder than intended, needing her sister to repeat the words. In reality, she didn't want to hear the words, yet she had longed for them her whole life. Perhaps she should just ignore Beverly and pretend sleepiness.

Then Bevvy pinched her arm and looked at their father. "Shush," she hissed.

Anne's stomach flopped. She spared her arm a brief glance, then focused on Gerald. If their father had heard, he gave no indication. His eyes had slanted into half slits, showing him on the verge of sleep.

Confirming their father paid no attention, Bevvy leaned in closer, as though using Anne's shoulder as a cushion for sleep. "Now I have a choice."

Anne dipped her chin and spoke from the corner of her lips. "A choice?" Her heart hammered with intensity, and a ringing had begun in her ears. She didn't know if she'd be able to hear her sister's answer.

"Just this night, Rathmore has declared himself to me. He says the engagement contract can be broken, as Garrett has been gone these many years." She stifled a giggle. "We've been thrust together these many months and find we are much suited. I will marry for love, my Anne. For love."

"What choice? Break the contract? Father will never allow it." Anne found herself mesmerized in confusion. Perhaps she was too tired to concentrate, and her heart was playing with her mind and creating a scenario she had only imagined possible. Truly, she could no longer understand the words. Yes, she'd heard Rathmore's name many times in passing, and had seen them dance amicably, but to ever consider their father would change his mind... "What are you talking about?"

Bevvy pinched her again. "Shush. Not now. Later."

Chapter Seven

Later came the next afternoon with its much screaming and tears, their father as unmoving as her sister, leaving Anne to bear witness as Harriet fretted and tried to appease both sides.

This couldn't be happening. How could Beverly have encouraged Rathmore? Her sister? The one person in the household always so quick to scold and hold Anne to what was expected and in keeping with decorum? Really, she must be dreaming. The last thing she remembered with any sense was when she had entered the garden. Perhaps she had sustained a head injury, as she now felt like she'd entered an alternate version of her everyday life.

Anne had spent the majority of her days avoiding this kind of contact. Other than family meals, they saw very little of their father, and she now wanted nothing more than to escape down to old Gavin Dun's apothecary in the village. There she could be herself. There she could learn and assist with the drying and bottling of his herbal concoctions. But in this moment of need, she could not abandon Bevvy. Bevvy would never abandon her if it were Anne in a face-off with their father.

Worse, though, and Anne felt her face flame, was she could not contain her stunning curiosity at the turn of events. Her mind, like a volcano, overflowed with the wonder of the circumstances and how each party would address the change. She could only be grateful that she was in the role of support and not the focus.

As if on a schedule he and Beverly had predetermined, Henry Rathmore had arrived after tea to formally request Beverly's hand. While Anne and Beverly spied from the landing above the drawing room, Henry addressed their father in uncharacteristic frankness, stating that he knew of the previous contract assigned to Garrett McGuire and requested it be terminated.

"What cheek," Anne barely whispered, agog with the audacity of someone daring to confront their father's decision in such a manner. "He'll be lucky if Father does not throw him from the grounds."

"Shush." Beverly's hands tightened within Anne's and her breath pulled in with a sharp whistle. "He must will out. I must have him."

Anne had never seen Beverly so fragile. She wondered if she had ever known her sister until now. This woman huddled next to her bore little to no resemblance to the vivacious, confident creature who normally ruled this house.

Fingers clasped tight to his hat, which hovered like a buoy near his middle, Henry took a step farther toward Gerald. "I offer land and station, and more importantly stability. Your daughter will want for nothing."

White-knuckled and in a voice which shook, he continued bravely on while in Gerald's stony presence. "My prospects are just as good as those of McGuire. As heir, I have a title to offer, plus the added advantage of familiarity with Miss Beverly."

When her father advanced a step at the notion of familiarity, Henry quickly amended. "I only mean, sir, we have been much thrown together in the company of our peers and have much in common." He elaborated on their growing friendship and conversations of the past year at balls and other social events.

Gerald retreated farther into the room, where his features remained visible only because he seemed to glow with high color. Though Henry's words seemed to soothe her father somewhat, to the point where his complexion softened from a puce back to a deep red with purple etchings. Had her fingers not been entwined with her sister's, Anne was sure she'd have bitten the nails to the quick during this encounter.

Gerald stalked about the room, his head bowed, hands behind his back. His boots banged with every step, causing an echo in the unnaturally quiet house. Like a bear they'd once seen on exhibit, he shook his head from side to side as he stalked the perimeter.

At last he stopped, braced his hands on his hips, and faced Rathmore. "No, it cannot be done."

"Surely you will not give your daughter to a man who is no better than a pirat—"

"Measure your words carefully." Gerald's icy tone cut across Rathmore's. His eyes seemed to bulge from their sockets.

Anne's estimation of Henry grew. It took a brave man to brace against the storm of Gerald.

"Brave or stupid," Anne said lightly in wonder.

"What?" Beverly breathed into her ear.

Anne patted her sister's hand and lifted her chin in the direction of the study. "Listen."

"Yes. Please excuse me." Rathmore drew an

51

audible breath and turned the hat in his hands. "I would ask only that you consider…"

Laying a palm along a volume on the bookshelf, Gerald did seem to contemplate further, for at least a moment. His fingers danced along the wood, a small staccato filling the space void of conversation. Family paintings, small miniatures, lined the shelf above. She didn't need to see what her father looked at to know where he stopped. She had memorized every item on that ledge since she'd been old enough to stand. At last, he paused on one of Anne as a baby in her mother's arms. She had no recollection of the moment it captured, though she treasured the piece dearly.

As he took the picture between his fingers, as though drawn, Anne disentangled herself from Beverly. She stepped from the vantage point, knowing without being able to articulate the how, of what was to come. Words of protest raced up her throat and amplified in her brain, yet she remained mute. Hand braced on the railing, she began her descent. This could not be. This would be the ruin of them all.

"Though our Beverly is not available…" Her father hadn't noticed Anne's approach. "As you know, she has been promised elsewhere. There is a contract. We are civilized human beings. The honoring of such things is what sets us apart. As a gentleman, you can understand, I cannot—will not—go back on my word," he said, a forced smile showing his crooked, stained teeth.

Rathmore looked poised to protest, but Gerald held up a palm, stilling the argument.

"I will grant, you do make a persuasive argument. An allegiance with the Rathmores would be a fine one. Due to the circumstances, it has never been considered.

Now I see it is nothing to be dismissed."

Anne's breath caught and held as she entered the room.

"I have, you know, two fine daughters." His smile struck Anne as foreign and as ingenuine as his words. "Though she is not so socially gifted as our Beverly, perhaps you will consider applying your affections to my youngest, Anne."

Anne gasped.

"No!" Beverly shouted from the landing and ran down the stairs into the drawing room.

Anne felt the floor swim beneath her. She laid a hand along the door casing to steady herself. "I will not do it," Anne said and turned, heart breaking, to see tears streaming down her sister's face. "I will not be given away in place of another."

"You cannot—"

"I can!" Her father raised his voice. He lifted his chin. "If Rathmore, here, will agree, we will draw up the papers."

Anne ached to reach out for her sister's hand. But there was no comfort to be had by either of them. Instead, she clenched them into fists. To be aligned with this hawk-nosed arrogant man who paid her as much attention as he would an annoying fly was too much to bear. She drew in her breath, knowing her color to be high from the heat on her skin, and measured each word as she had experienced Gerald do often to be heard.

"I will not."

Three pairs of eyes stared at her. Bevvy's face streamed with tears. Rathmore stood, his mouth agape, and her father opened and closed his mouth, then shook his head.

Anne turned and fled from the room, out the main door, across the lawn, and into the woods.

Chapter Eight

Garrett picked at the grass, then tossed a pebble with his free hand. Despite his lack of concentration, he had every intention of fishing. Alone. No one to bother or hound or question. No orders to give. No timeline to keep.

Often, he fished from his ship, but there it was competitive, the sailors betting on who would bring in the big one. Being back on the family property, he realized he missed the tranquility of sitting by a stream and allowing the lure to float atop the lazy current. In the past his father would join him, but he'd noticed a significant aging of his once-vibrant father since the last time they'd seen one another.

Sitting in the quiet, he struggled with the many dilemmas that hadn't seemed to exist mere weeks ago. He longed to return to his ship and the sea, but his father required him to run the business. Mack's ailing health brought to the surface Garrett's sorrow at losing his mother while still a lad. This further reminded him how he longed for a woman destined never to be his, while being saddled with another who clearly wanted nothing to do with him.

Leaning against a rock, surrounded by the thick bush and the bird song, he finally gave way to his exhaustion. The breeze seemed to caress as he dozed off. What seemed like only a moment later, the crashing of branches brought him back with a start. He sat up and dropped the rod, ears alert.

Attuned to a life fraught with danger, he remained still, listening to identify the source of what he heard. Unconcerned that there might actually be anything of concern on his own lands, instinct won out. Searching between the natural sounds of rustling leaves and the burbling brook, he waited. Perhaps a stag had been spooked. The quiet persisted and the birds had not resumed the song.

Retaining a sense of stealth, he retrieved the rod which had fallen from his hand and noted the pull on the line. Not a tugging to denote a fish. Likely a simple explanation of the string being caught on a reed or stone in the river's bed.

Readying himself to stand, he paused as a string of distinctive muffled curses traveled through the thicket. There, at last, had been what pulled him from a brief slumber. He yanked the line and it pulled free. The tension lessened as he coiled the string.

The thwack of a club against the trunk of a tree traveled on the air current of sound over the short distance to him. He estimated the person lay on the other side of a clump of rowan trees just tall enough to obscure his view. A villager, perhaps. Certainly no poacher would alert all to his presence.

Another round of cursing erupted from a distinctly feminine voice, with an added thump to the poor tree.

"What the bloody hell." He was sure the tree was undeserving of the abuse.

Garrett stowed the rod with his fishing kit to the side of the rock he had moments ago lounged against. Had the tavern owner's wife stomped onto their property to assault his trees with her anger? The village tavern owner had been well-known to sample too much of his own wares, which in turn led to his investigation of many a petticoat. Still, this was a matter to be left in house. If Garrett's memory served, his wife was a specimen far above what the portly man deserved, at any rate. She too should consider finding comfort elsewhere.

The trespassing irked rather than angered him. More the thought that who he had taken as a more high-born mistress was using the language of a bawdy woman made him curious. As he identified the current string of words, he felt his own cheek grow warm. This was a woman whose vocabulary would make his own crew blush.

Using a stealthy step, he worked his way through the thick bramble. The tirade continued and grew louder the closer he moved. Now, he wasn't sure of the identity. The voice struck him as younger pitched than he first imagined. A milk maid or perhaps a member of the traveling gypsies? Surely no one of any breeding would dare to speak such language aloud, even if they were alone.

He paused and his step faltered, identifying some of the names she was thoroughly cursing. Garrett couldn't believe his ears. By this point his Bessy had soundly committed everyone in her known circle, it seemed, to the seven realms of hell.

"By the bloody Lord Jesus himself, I shall be no man's second choice," she said, holding the bough like an axe and swinging it against the tree with the same breath. "Given away without thought or consideration for my own plans for the future."

What had possibly happened to put her in such a state? He must calm these hysterics before someone else was drawn by the noise.

"Anne Elizabeth MacLeod." He stood erect and strode into the clearing, no longer concealing his approach. His words were out before he realized he had spoken. "What in the name of all that is holy are you doing? And where in the creator's green acre did you learn such language?"

If her brother Brian were home, or worse yet, her father were to hear her now, she'd be soundly whipped and confined to her room, perhaps even sent to a nunnery. The female outburst was never tolerated for long. His own mother was said to have had quite the temper, though she had learned, over time, to appreciate the comforts of a lady. In her moments of agitation, his father always reminded him that she had grown up on the streets of Halifax town and had been taught no better. Mackenzie's second wife, Matilda, had been provided no such quarter. Neither was the case with his Bessy. Beverly had seen to her strict upbringing of decorum.

Anne started at the sound of his voice. She pivoted slightly on her heel, her mouth open, club raised in her hand. Her beautiful mossy-green eyes were squinted against the glare from the rays of sun shining directly upon her through the canopy of the branches. Her face, rosy with color, streamed with sweat. Her damp hair, long since loose of any confines, billowed around her head in corkscrew curls and the dun-colored dress was smeared with stains. What a sight to behold. She could be a Viking's mistress from the dark ages, set about on her own campaign of raids.

Anger blazed from every pore. In the intensity of her gaze, he noticed in the sunlight how flecks of gold shimmered there. Though she lowered the bough, she didn't seem to miss a beat, being neither afraid nor overly concerned that she'd been caught in her tirade.

"Who the bloody hell are you to preach at me, Garrett Mackenzie McGuire," she said, taking liberal use of his full name, as he had done with her, drawing each syllable out as she pointed the stick at him. "You come back here, fine as you please, with no thoughts to anyone else or the impact you have wrought on their lives, and have the impudence to call me out."

This was unexpected. Whatever could she mean? He and Beverly being promised was nothing new. "Bessy…" He ran his palm over the scruff of his chin. "Where in the blazes did you ever hear—"

"'Tis Anne." She stomped her small foot, making an indent in the soft earth. Color flared upon her cheeks like a burn. "I told you I am a child no more." She wrapped her free hand around the base of the branch and swung again. Leaves showered to the ground around her. "Do not presume to treat or talk to me as such."

He could see she was actually making a dent in the trunk. He blinked as the thud resounded around him. "I can see that," he said much lower than before. He could see where the cut on her palm from the night previous had opened up. A pink smear coated the wood where she held it firm. "You are right—Bes—Anne—I should not have made assumptions with my familiarity. 'Tis as you say, a long time since we were children running savage in these woods."

She pushed a damp lock from where it clung to her

59

cheek. "And don't try to get around me, either. 'Tis all your fault in any case, so there'll be no getting around it. No getting around any of it."

She swung again, but this time she missed and pirouetted, lost her balance and sank into the tall grass. There she bent in an ungraceful mess and covered her face in her hands, leaving tracks of mud and blood in the wake.

Garrett stood stunned for a moment. His fault? He hooked his thumbs in his trousers and leaned against the nearest tree trunk. What could possibly be his fault? He'd had nothing to do with her. Well, that wasn't exactly true, but surely assisting someone with a shoe couldn't have gotten her into trouble and certainly not to the extent of her outburst. Had she guessed his deeper feelings for her and projected her anger due to her affection for her sister? He'd felt he kept his feelings well buried.

As cautiously as he would approach a wild animal, arms outstretched, palms down, Garrett breached the distance, slowly. He knelt close but retained a distance so he didn't hover in his height. "I cannot be sure," he began in a modulated tone, "but I think I may need to bill you for the cost of the tree."

She lifted her gaze to him, eyes moist, her face a mask of confusion. "What?"

His attempt at humor crashed and was forgotten like the branch so recently used as a weapon. "My tree." He pointed. "You've used my tree most aggressively."

"*Your* tree?" She stood, like a firecracker being launched from a Chinese cannon, hands on her hips. "By the Lord Jesus, man, for all your years at sea, do you have no sense of direction?"

In that moment he felt grateful she had dropped the branch. Garrett gaped and stood too. How dare someone—insult his intelligence. His own anger flared bright. Of course he knew his own land. He'd played in these woods his whole youth. He glanced around the clearing, hearing the warble of the stream over the pounding of his own heart. Was she deranged in some way? Need he restrain her and bring her back to the manor for attending?

She took a step toward him, and he resisted the urge to step back at her intensity. He crossed his arms across his chest and took a deep breath. How could he possibly be intimidated by someone who barely crossed the height of five feet?

"As soon as you crossed that brook, you idiot..." She pointed toward the stream, then swept a hand across the clearing. "You stepped over onto MacLeod land. You are not yet married into our family. You are not yet master of all. And you will not tell me whose tree I abuse."

In the times he had allowed himself to remember Bessy, he'd always recalled fondly the wood-nymph kind of child who'd followed him and Brian, her joyous laughter, and her shy manner around strangers. She'd haunted his dreams with her grace and lit his imagination for her wonderment. Just who was this fiery creature before him now? He'd never seen her in such a rage. What had happened to her in these intervening years to create such a ferocious creature?

He was given no more time to ponder, as she stomped off, leaving him feeling like a rogue wave had just swamped the fine decks of his ship and threatened to capsize them in the midst of a storm.

He swept a hand across his brow and through his hair. "By all that is holy, what was that?"

Chapter Nine

Anne walked frantically for a quarter of an hour, keeping a pace that made sweat run down her spine. She kicked at roots and rocks along the way, anything to appease her insatiable anger. As though on a precipice, she had never felt so alone. No one would stand by her. Bevvy was powerless and their father unmoving.

Rathmore would either accept or reject. Either decision would ruin Anne. If he accepted, knowing his feelings for Beverly being mutual, her relationship with her sister would be at an end. If he rejected, Anne could only wonder what would be her fate.

Hacking her foot too deep into the foliage, at too much speed, she stubbed her toe and felt the jarring in her ankle as she came to an immediate stop. "Oh, my land," she muttered and bit her lip to stem the tears. She was fresh out of all the oaths she had learned in the village where the apothecary's shop backed onto the tavern.

A wave of embarrassment swept her as she hobbled a few paces, then stopped, panting. To think he'd been witness to her tirade. Would she ever live this down? At last, the pain overrode her frustrated anger and she had to lean against a tree. In these circumstances, with no options, she could do little but return home. But not like this. Glancing down, she

63

noticed the mud and bramble, pieces of twigs, and bracken stuck to various parts of her dress. Not to mention the smear of blood, and she could only imagine the state of her hair.

Never mind. She could go by way of the kitchen and up the back stairs to her room and change. Then…no, she couldn't face it. But she would have to. She'd have to face her father…and Beverly.

"No."

Tears stung and her throat ached where she tried to swallow them down. Gerald, her father, would want the match. Rathmore presented an opportunity to make a match that was too good to pass up. He would then have both his daughters strategically aligned. Her father couldn't have planned it better for Anne, knowing for a long time he'd felt at a loss for what to do with his strange daughter who preferred herbs and the woods to society, when the time came. She'd half imagined he expected her to become a spinster or someone to be placed in a nunnery.

"Bah."

Balanced on one foot, she lowered herself to the ground beneath a flowering dogwood bush. The soft fragrance gentled the jagged edges of her emotions. Taking her calf in one hand, with the fingers of her other, she first rotated the impacted toe and then probed the ankle. Nothing significant seemed amiss despite the throb of pain. She'd be fine. To be safe, though, she edged off her stocking and wrapped the foot carefully before slipping her sturdy shoe back on, leaving the laces loose.

Anne glanced to the sky, hoping for an answer in the swath of scuttling clouds. Why did he continue to call her the pet name of her youth? Could Garrett not see that she had grown? She might not be the sweeping beauty of her sister, but she was no child.

She hiccupped as the tears ran. She'd certainly acted the part of the child today. He, nor likely any other man, would ever see her as she wanted to be seen. Perhaps if she carried herself as Bevvy had instructed. Perhaps if she had learned how to make polite conversation and react to news as a lady. But Garrett's return had taken her completely unaware. Bevvy's reaction and declaration had swum out of the clear blue sky, and her father's barter with Henry…

"No." But the word was barely a hush in the breeze.

She couldn't run away. No one could help her. Women had no say in such things. All would agree the match a good one and that it was her duty as a daughter to be obedient. If her father determined Henry Rathmore to be the best choice and Rathmore was willing to take her on, Anne had to submit. Her prospects, of which there were none, offered little else for consideration.

But to be married to a man she knew preferred her sister? How miserable and awkward would her relationship with her sister be after such an arrangement! As much as she adored and loved Beverly, she could not imagine being wed under such circumstances. She'd rather be sent to the nunnery.

The convent, where she'd likely never see her family again. Never have an opportunity to see Garrett, even as a brother-in-law, from afar.

She stood and stifled a sob. Measuring her weight across her stance, she stepped into the bush. Plucking

65

some blossoms from the plant, avoiding the prickles, she made her way much more slowly to the stream. Pausing by the water's edge, she decided to clean up as best she could. There would be a reckoning, no doubt, as soon as she returned, and she should at least be prepared in event her escape up the back stairs became thwarted.

Pebbles dug into her knees through the layers of her bunched skirts as she hovered above the water. Like the spritz of a perfume, the faint odor of lilac tantalized. She scanned the brush for the source, then noticed the face reflected off the rippling water. Hideous and dirty, and he'd seen her like this. She set about her ablutions. Humiliation mounted, burning her skin. Where had the optimism from the ball gone? In so little time her life had flattened in available opportunities. Was that only last night when she felt the tingle from his touch on her calf? The forbidden wanting curling in her stomach?

Anger returned, and she bunched her fists and slammed them into the water. Would today never end? She splashed her face and her hair to the point that, when she was done, her clothing hung heavy and drenched. Sitting back on her haunches, careful of her bruised foot, she concentrated on the sway of the trees and the breath of the breeze, slowing her reaction to match the tempo. She combed her fingers through her hair until the tangles had been smoothed. On impulse, she threaded the wild roses around her crown and felt better. Childlike. Perhaps she could pretend, just for the length of the trek home, she were a child again with little to concern herself so long as she remained in the woods.

Standing, she ran her hands along her dress, doing

her best to ease the wrinkles. "'Tis no use," she muttered. "No use at all." She wasn't a child, and her life had never been carefree, so pretending became moot.

Turning back to the path, she started, heart thudding in one awful jolt in her chest. Her hand flew to her mouth to stifle the cry, while the other clutched her middle.

"You always did have a good sense of direction," Garrett said, standing with his hands on his hips, his clothes looking as matted or worse than her own with stains. His stare was almost predatory as he raked her with his dark eyes from head to toe.

Then he smiled. His grin, slightly lopsided with only one of his dimples visible, struck her as slightly shy. He kicked at a stone, which skittered only a few feet to his left. He stepped toward her. "On board ship, I depend on my first mate to navigate. When it is up to me, I use my instruments and am guided either by the angle of the sun or the position of the stars."

His voice had taken on a husky timbre, and the hair at the nape of her neck rose as though he had whispered a breath across her skin. Regaining her breath with effort, though her heart continued to hammer, Anne crossed her arms over her chest, feeling the press of her nipples against the damp fabric. As she did, a soft pink petal slid down across her cheek, making her aware of the flowers in her hair. She ached to pull them free and toss them aside. Curling her hands into fists under her arms, she resisted the impulse. Then she felt the chill of the breeze through her damp clothing, now that her anger had dissipated and the wind had picked up.

He took another step closer, and she could smell

the sweet scent of the trees and grass coming off his skin. She ached, as she never did before, to trail her fingers along his cheek, to feel the stubble of his beard now shadowing his square jaw.

"I guess I ran these woods so often with Brian that one side of the river to the other meant little to me then. But…" He swept a forelock off his brow and kicked at another rock, bringing him so close his breath fanned her forehead.

"Marriage."

He paused and swallowed, and she watched his adam's apple bob.

"A marriage is to unite the families. This is your father's land now and will be Brian's in the future. I want you to know…"

His voice trailed off, his gaze shifting from the ground to meet hers as fierce as a collision across the distance. His palms came up and caressed her hot cheeks, his full lips only as far away as their noses.

"Need you to know…that it is not my intention… never has been—"

Anne dropped her hands to her sides. "What *is* your intention?"

With a soft caress, he tilted her head and his lips brushed hers. Her stomach clenched and released, and a deep throb filled her core. She felt the kiss run across the nerve endings to the fiber of her being.

He leaned back a fraction. His dark blue eyes bore into hers before he leaned in again and the kiss deepened. Her lips parted and his tongue smoothly stroked hers. She had never imagined. No one had ever told her.

How could Beverly choose the arrogant Henry

Rathmore over Garrett McGuire? Guilt and anger blazed again, radiating through her like a torch to dry tinder. She stepped back, her hand covering her lips where he had seemed to bring her life where she hadn't known there was dormancy.

How could she have allowed this? How could he have taken such liberty? Of course, based on her previous behavior, he would think he could. She had brought this on herself. She would be ruined.

He stared at her a long moment, nodded, and stepped back.

Her breath came in shallow pants, leaving her feeling she would never breathe easy again. Under his intense scrutiny she blinked several times, conscious of her clothing, disheveled hair, the grime that the stream could not make clean. She knew it then as surely as if Garrett had said the words out loud. She could never be anything next to the great beauty of her sister. How dare she covet what wasn't hers.

"I thought I knew," he finally said, dropping his hands to his sides as though defeated. "But it seems, I don't really know. Nothing at all, any more. My ship is home to me now, and I'd like nothing better than to return to her and set sail."

Anne too dropped her hands to her sides, confused and exhausted by the day's events. "Then you should go." Why had he not automatically said his intention was to be married to her sister? She shook her head and met his gaze, daring him to deny her next words. "For she doesn't want you anyway."

She intended to turn and leave, but looked over her shoulder. "You've brought nothing but misery, Garrett McGuire, and your ship and men are welcome to you.

Because of your return and the decisions of others, I will be stuck marrying a man in love with my sister, where you can only find affection for lumber parceled together to float upon the vast ocean like a leaf on this stream."

Anne heaved a great gulp of air, then bit her lip to prevent further disgrace. For a moment, she studied the storm of emotions which seemed to mirror her own but on his firm features. He opened his mouth, only to close it again, then raised a hand as though to finally speak, but Anne, realizing she had said far too much, revealed too much, threatened her father's plans, fled the clearing.

If only a burial plot lay close at hand, she would have made use of the opportunity to allow the earth to swallow her. Bunching her skirt in her hands to raise the heavy fabric above her knees, she fled as fast as she could for the manor despite the ache in her foot.

****

Much later, clean and freshly dressed, her hand bandaged, her foot swaddled, with her soiled garments tucked away in a corner behind the armoire, Anne had composed herself enough to sit calmly, though there was very little inside that was calm. She was a tempest in the ocean, her mind living and reliving the kiss.

Like a statue, she was frozen into immobility by the obscenity of her disregard for her sister. Had it been Bevvy's declaration for Rathmore that had finally freed her guilt? She couldn't say what had come over her to allow such a liberty, and by Garrett, of all people.

How she'd made it back to the manor unseen was a miracle. The small victory did little to elevate her growing anxiety over what would come from her blunder. Forcing her legs into submission, she crossed the room to the mirror. With light fingers, conscious of where his mouth had brushed hers, she pulled her lip back from her teeth to inspect the damage. A white indentation showed where she'd bitten hard against the strain of emotion to the point where she'd drawn blood.

It had been a fortunate thing that she hadn't been seen or stopped when she wound through the back kitchen garden alternately cursing and praying in pain and panic. How could she have blurted such a thing and run off? The situation had been bad enough, based on the day's events, but now the storm escalated to hurricane proportions with her revelation to Garrett. What would he do? By the lord above, what would happen to Bevvy? Would Garrett call Rathmore out? Once he found out about her telling Garrett, her father would surely disown Anne.

Stomach knotted, she walked to the window and gripped the sill. She sighed heavily. Then stood straight. She wasn't alone in her misery. Her sister's sobs could be heard through the walls. What was to become of them now?

Chapter Ten

Stunned not only by the revelation but by his own actions, Garrett marched home heedless of the water slopping over the tops of his boots as he traversed the stream. It was surely one thing to imagine his having to marry her sister, but quite another to have to picture his Bessy married off to someone else. He had never allowed for such contemplation in his thoughts of her before.

Anne and Henry. It could not be. It would not be.

Had he imagined her response to him? Today only served to prove Anne to be his match in all ways. Her bold audacity in confronting him. The wild display of freedom—that she would take her liberty and be bound by no one—it equaled his own quest for freedom. Then there was the ease of being in her own presence, which corresponded to his own. Where she continued to shy from social events, he'd learned to adapt.

"That will come," he said, winding through the trailing vines, attracted by the savory smells of roasting meat emitted by the cook's kitchen. The taste of her still on his tongue, he couldn't contain a fleeting smile.

This quickly soured as he pictured what her life would be like saddled to a dandy like Rathmore. Made worse by all the while knowing the man preferred and had requested her sister's hand. The thought was enough to sour his hunger. But wait...could there be an opportunity therein? Had she not said that Beverly wanted Rathmore equally? Had she not confirmed Beverly loathed the match to him as much as he?

His step slowed and he scuffed the heel of his boot on the gravel. Having seen enough family-enforced marriages, Garrett didn't require a crystal ball to predict what his or Anne's future would look like if things proceeded on their current course. An heir and spare and then a husband lusting and whoring, too dim-witted to hide the infidelity, and societal circles accepting this as the normal turn of events.

He didn't differentiate himself from Rathmore in that capacity. Four people, each promised to the wrong person. Was this his fate with Beverly? Hadn't he already resigned himself, with the consolation he'd always have his ship and the sea?

Now, like the flicker of a single candle in a dark room, the light of Anne and the memory of their kiss seemed enough to propel him onward.

****

Mackenzie MacGuire stood in the doorframe questioning Garrett. "To London?"

Garrett accepted his overcoat from the butler, and after shrugging it across his broad shoulders, took his hat and secured it firmly over his brow. "Yes, Father," he replied as he moved toward the door. "I have some business to attend to."

"Family business?" His father pulled the spectacles from the end of his nose and dangled them off the tips of his fingers. His once-jet hair was now more gray than black, though he continued to wear it queued as he had when captaining the ship. "Why wasn't I made aware?"

73

Garrett paused, his boots resounding on the polished wood. Though he'd been in charge of the shipping portion of the business for many years, his father retained a significant hold over their day-to-day affairs. He brushed a hand across his forearm to clear an unseen speck.

Despite the inflexibility Mackenzie exhibited for the insistence on the union with the MacLeods, Garrett held a strong respect for his father, and they had always shared a fond friendship beyond the scope of paternity. His father's strong stand in this matter of the marriage Garrett always attributed more to Mackenzie wanting to abide by Flora's final wish for her only son.

"Your intention is for me to take over, in all ways, the family business. As you so often point out, in order to do that, I must become familiar with our holdings." He inclined his chin a fraction to suggest the question over the statement of fact. "I've an appointment with Watkins, our solicitor, to review the books, become familiar with our assets, and see where we can grow and expand with our ever-increasing presence in the Americas."

The smile which transformed Mackenzie's face, and brought back some of his lost youth and vigor, took Garrett unexpectedly. He wasn't exactly lying to his father, but more failing to expand on the truth—the family business being an excuse, while his intention had everything to do with the notion his Bessy had seeded in his mind.

"At last," his father said, crossing the space between them and slapping Garrett on the back. Stepping back, he repositioned his glasses on his nose. He clapped a hand against his thigh. "I shall set the dinner with the MacLeods for a fortnight, and we shall make the formal announcement then."

Garrett nodded once, his stomach tight with anticipation, mingling with dread as he stepped over the threshold. The clock had begun to tick.

****

It had begun to rain during his journey. Despite shedding his overcoat, damp still drenched his hair, and several times he'd had to swipe rivulets out of his eyes, blinking to clear his vision. Striving to stay calm and not give away his inner emotion, Garrett stood from his seat by the desk and walked to the window.

"All I'm asking is, Watkins, is…is it possible?" Garrett paced the wood-paneled room, made darker over the years by its owner's constant smoking. "A simple yes or no would suit."

Elbow rested on the desktop, Russell Watkins rubbed two fingers under a bulbous nose the color of a ripe plum from his love of spirits. A sparse moustache decorated his lip like a shadow. The man's globular, bloodshot eyes traced Garrett's progress back and forth as he seemed to consider the question. "Umm, well."

The silence stretched, each second punctuated by the heels of his boots echoing off the wood, drawing Garrett's unease ever closer to the surface. Here was his chance, perhaps his only opportunity to change his fate and yet still uphold his promise to his father. He could see a future with Anne—his Bessy. Could see it as clearly as he could the next building across the street. There had to be a way.

He couldn't go back. He'd locked the idea as he did a course on his ship, his aim and destination clear. While he negotiated his plan these last couple of days in the city, in those darkest hours before the dawn, when his resolve was at its weakest, he couldn't help allowing his imaginings to whisper to her across the marriage bed.

He mustn't get ahead of himself. Jamming a hand into his pocket, he strode to stand level at the end of the wide desk and bent to lay a palm atop the contract. He glowered intently at the man who held his fate in his legal hands. Watkins had had time enough to resolve the issue. It either was or wasn't, and he'd have to deal with either, but he must know.

Never one to be intimidated, Garrett knew Watkins, Esquire, had dealt with his share of murderers, thieves, and the politically connected gentry. The likes of Garrett Mackenzie McGuire was unlikely to impart any sway to a man like this if the law would not permit it. This had been a significant factor of consideration when Garrett had decided to retain Watkins during his secession from his father. While many of his peers suggested a new lawyer and not one so used to the senior McGuire, Garrett respected the man personally and professionally and knew no other could compare. Still, that didn't stop Garrett from trying to impose his own will.

Icy blue eyes stared back unwaveringly and unintimidated for only a few heartbeats before a small crook of the lips dislodged the fingers and set Watkins to action. He drew the sheaf of papers toward him, dropping his gaze from Garrett to flip to a particular passage.

"There is no specific reference to one MacLeod daughter over the other." He skimmed his finger over one page and then the other.

Garrett drew air in through his nose, aware he'd been breathing too shallowly. He swallowed back the lump that had formed in his throat.

The lawyer continued. "You're asking for a proxy, of sorts." He lifted his salt-and-pepper brows and re-piled the stack. "Have one stand in for the other?"

Garrett didn't much care for the reference, but if it achieved his end, he wouldn't argue. Still, a bit confused, he shrugged, then shook his head. "No," he said, drawing out the word, pinching his lips together. "If I understand, a proxy denotes that the original still stands as the bride. Casts the vote, as it were, for the original." He shook his head again, straightened, and hooked his thumbs in his waistband. "I want to replace one with the other."

Watkins released a sigh, which seemed as close as he ever came to a chuckle. "I'll say this much for you, McGuire—just when I thought I had seen everything I could see, you've brought me something new."

Garrett strode to the fireplace and leaned a shoulder against the rock mantel. "Can it be done?"

Watkins dropped the papers to the tabletop and leaned back in his chair to brace his hands behind his head. "Is this—" His gaze shifted to his notes. "—Anne Elizabeth willing?"

Garrett turned to stare into the fire, as much to contemplate as to hide his features from scrutiny. True, this was a gamble on his part. Perhaps Anne would think no better of his proposal than she had of the thought of being fostered onto Rathmore. Yet he knew. How? The sane side of his brain wondered. What indications had she given that she would accept him? A fleeting kiss that he had imposed on her?

"Doesn't matter," he muttered into the flames. He just knew.

"You risk losing everything." Watkins echoed his thought. "The older sister may feel thwarted, her reputation ruined—"

"The contract isn't public."

"Still, have you considered, you pit one sister against the other."

"Beverly doesn't want me," Garrett said, turning to face the barrister. "I'm giving her a way out."

"I don't profess to know ladies like I know the law, but I know this much," he said, tilting his head farther back and seeming to gaze up to the soot-stained ceiling. "It's one thing for a woman to not want you and make that decision herself, quite another when the man decides for her."

Chapter Eleven

Garrett hadn't bothered to alert his father to his decision. As he approached the MacLeod manor, a brief pang of guilt fizzled, then died. Until he knew the outcome, why engage in further conversation. The reality was that he didn't want to have to examine this nor explain himself out loud while still trying to figure it out himself, all the while questioning his means and motives.

He almost felt like a misbehaving child, yet he'd been in command of a ship for quite some time, and needing his father's approval seemed counterproductive to his intentions. Still, as he removed his coat and hat and settled in the drawing room waiting for Gerald to appear, a war of emotions and doubts raged.

His future father-in-law approached him warmly, clasping his hand between both his own. There seemed no hint of the upheaval Anne had revealed only days before. Perhaps the family had settled, Anne and Beverly resigned to their fate. But as Garrett reached inside his breast pocket and pulled from it a copy of the contract, he didn't think he imagined a flicker of apprehension.

As he sat across the heavy desk from Gerald, he strove to keep the tremor from his fingers when he laid the revised contract, notarized, flat on the polished oak. Perhaps he should have brought his father along. Even at his age, the man was still the most imposing person Garrett knew. If ever he needed an ally, this was the moment.

Settling back, he laid his hands lightly on the armrests. He refused to give in to his inclination to grip them in order to keep from fidgeting. This kind of anxiety, foreign to his current daily life of command, was like reliving a memory from a long-forgotten dream. The last time he'd been this nervous was when his father took him to town for the first time to make a man out of him.

Only managing to half listen as Gerald mumbled his way through the revised documents, Garrett rolled his gaze to the ceiling. His pulse ticked too loudly, and his ears rang with the strain of composure. Perhaps he'd gone about this all wrong. Would his actions cause irreparable damage? Should he have held a meeting with Watkins present as well as both his father and Gerald? Certainly in this moment, he would have imparted more sway if he'd brought Watkins along. The two of them could have persuaded Gerald to the logic of the plan. Gerald's present course seemed likely to destroy the family rather than bind as had been the original intention of the mothers.

Surely the man could see the futility of saddling Beverly with a man she didn't want to marry. Making an offer for Anne in her stead would fix everything. Provided, of course, she would have him. Garrett had determined, during the last two days in the city, that regardless of Gerald's or his father's consent, he would not marry a woman unwilling to the match. The contract had been modified, but even so, he would destroy it and leave the country, never to return, if that was the outcome—if Anne be unwilling.

Gerald rose from his chair with a grunt, the document in his large hand, and began to pace.

"Is Mack aware of this?"

"No, sir," Garrett said on a swallow. "He is not. I felt it only right not to presume but to speak to you first."

"Ah." The older man stopped his pacing and lowered his spectacles on his bulbous nose. "But you did not speak to me first, as you say. You consulted a lawyer first. Pray, tell me, lad, what is the problem with my fair Beverly that you seek to replace her…" He glanced at the page, raising his glasses, only to allow them to slip again when he pierced Garrett with a stony stare. "By a proxy, as you so eloquently put it here, and have that proxy be my younger daughter?"

Garrett had anticipated this very question. On the ride back from London, astride his beloved Rayne, a Byerly Turk Garrett had brought back from one of his journeys and housed, while he was at sea, in his father's ample stables, he considered what he might answer. He weighed out many options, while being ever cautious of revealing too much. First, he wasn't supposed to be in the know about Beverly's pining for the titled Henry Rathmore. He would never betray Anne's trust by stating where he'd learned of that. Instead, he could say he'd observed them together at the ball and saw how well matched they were. Second, neither he nor Beverly had any affections for one another. Anyone who had ever seen them could detect their coolness. And, like a mathematical question—third, the revised contract seemed the logical approach. Considering the first two, the revision offered a reasonable alternative that would be mutually beneficial to all parties concerned.

He nodded to himself, pleased to have foreseen the reasonable quarrel. Crossing one booted foot over the polished leather of the other, he smiled congenially.

"You have two wonderful daughters—"

Gerald snorted, interrupting Garrett's prepared beginning. The older man rolled the papers into a cylinder and shifted the bundle between thumb and forefinger, encircling the scroll.

Garrett cleared his throat and started again. "Your daughters are a credit to you, Mister MacLeod. Any man would be pleased to be called your son."

"Except you."

"Certainly not true at all," Garrett countered, keeping his voice level.

"What did you witness at the ball which changed your mind?" Gerald sat back in his chair, retaining his hold on the papers. "Did Anne say something to you? She can be erratic. I have never understood her and her infatuation with the herbalist—never mind that now. Why would you choose Anne over Beverly?"

"It is not my intention to suggest any lack at all in one or the other." He forced a smile to curl his lips. "When our mothers, these ladies…" He measured his words. "These great friends and distant cousins themselves had the contract drafted, it was to formalize the union of families reunited after having been separated when my own mother's parents moved to the new world."

Gerald snorted. "There is no denying the color your mother brought to any gathering. Sometimes I think she and Anne were cut from the same cloth, and wonder what in my late wife's bloodline seeped into our Anne."

Garrett had considered that marvel as well and smothered the emerging grin. "As I understand the intent, Mister MacLeod, it was to unite."

"Yes. So." Gerald released a sigh and laid the papers and his palm on the desk. "Do get to the point. This flowering on is wearing my patience."

"Anyone could see Beverly and Henry Rathmore had been much thrown together in my absence and have not only become acquainted but are indeed well suited."

"Surely you are not a jealous man, McGuire," Gerald said, rising to his feet yet again and rounding the desk to stand before Garrett. "I've no idea how you arrived at your notions. Who have you been speaking to? Did Rathmore approach you?"

Garrett rose as well, yet retained a respectable distance. Anne had been right.

"Surely not," Gerald continued. "How have you arrived at this…" He pointed down at the contract. "'Twas a ball, after all, and the ladies do like to dance. Tongues will wag and all that. We cannot deny them the simple pleasures of a social gathering. If Rathmore assumed more, you let me deal with him."

Garrett found his deck stacked with additional cards he hadn't anticipated. "So, I am not the first to broach this subject."

Gerald's lips thinned in answer.

"Am I to understand that Henry Rathmore would like their friendship to be more…formalized?" He allowed the last word to draw itself out.

Gerald hooted a bark of laughter which neither resembled amusement nor lit any merriment in his direct gaze. "Come now, McGuire. Have you spies amongst my household?" He looked around the study conspiratorially. "They misinform. The interest of another only increases the value of the prize. Beverly is trained and will be an asset. Anne remains a child and no match for a man already in command of a ship and on the verge of taking control of the family coffers."

Had Gerald taken the time these last years to notice the blossom of his youngest? Apparently not. Garrett bit back his initial response and held his jaw rigid. "No one can deny both the beauty and accomplishment of *both* your daughters, sir."

He let his words hang, unwilling to jeopardize his proposal by saying too much. He was far too close. Gerald had shown his hand by not denying Rathmore's intention. For the sake of the revised contract, let his preference not show and the sisters be considered equal and therefore pose no loss to Gerald MacLeod's pride.

"Tell me, now. Has Rathmore approached you?" Gerald braced his hands, fisted at his sides, knuckles white, betraying the depth of his emotion which his features managed to conceal. Not waiting for an answer, he retrieved the now crumpled stack of papers and stalked to the bookshelf.

Garrett heard the paper wrinkle in his fist.

Turning, Gerald faced him again, his brow creased, closing the distance between hairline and moss-green eyes which so resembled Anne's. "I did not encourage his suit and forbade Beverly from seeing him since."

Garrett raised a palm, sensing the tables turning in his favor. "Mister MacLeod," Garrett began, assuming a familiar tone, one he had used often enough these last years in bargaining deals while abroad. "It is not my intention to harm or wound. We are men of this world, and this is but a transaction. A business deal. And we all know a successful deal is made better when all parties are willing."

He drew a breath, his gaze sweeping the room, and noticed the open door. How had he not remembered to shut it? But Gerald had been the last to enter.

"Point of fact, sir," he continued, "we all want this union to work. You are a fortunate man, with two daughters, and thereby have provided your eldest with a choice. It is obvious by what you say that they have mutual intentions." He lowered his hand and shook his head, giving Gerald no room for denial. He pointed his chin toward the contract held tight in Gerald's grip. "For the sake of my mother…"

"And theirs." Gerald's face softened. "'Twas the fondest wish of the ladies. Great friends to the end, they were."

Garrett nodded. He could taste the victory and strained not to let it show.

"Taken far too soon," Gerald continued and rubbed a knuckle under one eye. "By thunder, both…far too soon."

"So you see," Garrett said, allowing his breath to ease out with the words. "I want a wife who wants to be a wife to me. A mother to our children. 'Tis of no use to force a union. It won't last."

Gerald's head shifted to the side. "Yet you think it would with Anne?"

"I've no way to know." Garrett turned and laid a hand atop the chair, averting his face so as not to give anything away. Maintaining a level voice, he continued. "But, as I understand, Anne has not had the interest of another, nor, to my knowledge, has another expressed an interest."

85

"So you do have spies." Gerald's voice hardened again. "If Rathmore had not approached you, how would you know such things?"

"No, sir, I assure you. No spies." Damnation, he must watch his words. "Just eyes in my head, able to see. Ears willing to listen."

Garrett let the silence hang in a question unasked, waiting for Gerald to concede and confirm the truth of the assumption.

Eventually, the other man nodded, unrolled the parchment as he strode across the room to again lay it flat on the desk. His hands braced against a stomach which would not stay put behind his belt. "'Tis correct," he affirmed. "Our Anne was not promised. Nor has she appeared interested, though…"

An angry flutter in Garrett's gut rippled outward and threatened the little candle of hope he had kindled during the discussion. He did not like the direction of the discussion being in the past tense.

Gerald turned to the decanters on a side table and poured amber liquid into each of two glasses. Handing one to Garrett, he raised the other to his lips, then hesitated. "Though…"

"Though?" Garrett echoed.

"Rathmore offers a good suit. He may not be as wealthy, but they are no paupers, and he comes complete with a title."

"Are you bargaining, sir?" Garrett agreed with a nod of his head. "Yes, Rathmore offers a titled advantage for your family on all accounts. However, if he had already spoken for Beve—"

"I have confirmed no such thing." Color dusted Gerald's almond-textured skin. Then he shook his head, and his complexion resumed a more normal hue. He raised his glass. "It seems we were of a common mind, then. All parties willing. There is no use to the pretense. You should know that when I declined Rathmore's interest in Beverly...I offered Anne."

Like a gunshot, Garrett felt he'd lost control of the negotiation. He drew a long breath and wished for a cheroot as something to occupy his hands other than the delicate glass. Just as Anne had surmised. He should have taken heed of her concern and trusted she would know the mind of her own father. Swallowing, he struggled to formulate the words to ask the question. "Have they agreed and set down the terms?"

"By God, I haven't. And I won't."

At the unexpected interruption, he and Gerald spun toward the sound. His drink sloshed and the glass almost fell to the floor. Framed in the doorway stood a specter of a slip of a girl, grown to a woman seemingly overnight. Feet planted, Anne faced the two men and seemed to stand ten feet tall. Her flushed face only highlighted the green of her eyes now ablaze in anger.

"I am not chattel to be bartered away at your whim." Gone were the angry hysterics he'd witnessed in the woods. This was a woman prepared to battle. Without shouting, her voice carried easily across the room, each syllable measured. Her hands gripped her hips. "I know my own mind, and hell or high water, I will live to *choose* my husband."

She was gone before Garrett remembered to close his mouth, so shocked he was by the outburst and the flame of the woman he intended to marry. His loins tightened as he imagined fusing with such passion. If only it could be directed at him.

Gerald, by contrast, turned to Garrett, hand mopping down his face. "Where…" he began, then stopped. "Where on Earth did she learn such language?"

Chapter Twelve

She'd done it again. Made a fool of herself in front of the one man she wanted never to see her a fool.

Where had all this rage come from? Beverly had asked her the same question just that morning.

"Your whole life, my dear sister, you could always be relied upon to be so meek and mild," she said, drawing Anne into her embrace. "We neither of us should be surprised by father's actions and choices. We have always known his intent."

She had missed her sister's counsel these last days, but what could they say to one another? Certainly Beverly had always known who she was promised to and what life would be, and had seemed resigned to accept her circumstances. But Anne had pictured a different outcome if she ever allowed her imaginations to emerge. At the moment she couldn't recall how she had pictured her life with Garrett McGuire, but she knew she'd never imagined life with another.

Anne's rage quickly morphed into embarrassment as she spun from the library door and saw Bevvy standing as though transfixed on the stairwell opposite. Mortified, she fled the house, intent on the only safe place she knew—the woods, the wild plants, the birds.

Did Beverly not know of Rathmore's proposal? Surely she must. Perhaps she did know and was willing to allow Rathmore to go, and accept Garrett and a life of regret that was sure to follow. However, Anne was sure, in that moment, Bevvy had no idea of her father's intention for Anne, and her heart ached on what that knowledge would do to their relationship, their bond as sisters.

Heart pounding, she hoisted her skirts and ran. Rounding the corner of the kitchen garden, she tripped on a wayward tomato vine and lay sprawled and winded for a long moment, listening for pursuers. Why, even in this moment, could she not be graceful?

Confusion reigned. She knew everything and knew nothing all at once. Her mind spun in a million directions, and she breathed deeply to get her bearings. As Brian would always say to her, "In order to know where you are going and how to get there, you must first know where you are." Anne centered her soul, knowing she was not willing to accept her sister's discarded beaus, nor was she willing to give up so easily and be exchanged like livestock.

Getting to her knees, still lower than the berry bushes along the outer edge of the vegetable patch, she peered through the shrubbery. Heavy footfalls tramped on the cobbles, and she scooted farther into the shadows. Dank earth and the mixed pleasant aromas of bounty beckoned. How she longed for when her life had been significantly less complicated, when she could freely go to town and learn from the old herbalist. Was that only days ago? Ever since Garrett McGuire had returned, her life had been thrown into turmoil.

If only she could set aside her own response. Better if she could forget that kiss, but her lips continued to tingle every time she recalled the moment and the tenderness.

The tenor of male voices sailed across the distance. Truly, if she didn't want to be treated like a child, as Bevvy would say, she had to stop acting like one. However, in this moment, pulse racing and stomach clenched, she peered from the gloom, unable to face another living soul.

Garrett's height and confident march gave away his identity, despite the distance. The mere sight of him filled her with that blasted longing mixed equally with anger.

Her father and Garrett conversed in low tones as they covered the grounds, Garrett bending his head to be more level with her father. She couldn't distinguish any of their words. Then they passed, leaving only the buzzing of insects behind.

Anne chided herself for acting the part of the infant and hiding. If only she were a man, she'd be in control of her own destiny. She would take what she wanted. Beverly had tried to sway her father in her mature, graceful fashion, and he would not be budged. As that didn't work, Anne saw no need for her try any other way than what she had. Surely, when it came to it, she could not be forced. She simply would decline at the altar, and that was that.

Confident she would not be discovered, she stood close to the raspberry bushes and watched the two men depart in the opposite direction. That struck Anne as strange, and she raised a hand to shelter her eyes and peered after them. Garrett would know exactly where to find her if he wished to find her. She'd haunted the same woods as he and Brian since they were children. Perhaps, she suspected, he didn't wish to find her. Maybe her removal fit better with his plans.

But why did he kiss her?

She stroked her index finger across her lower lip. This uncertainty gave her pause. Garrett did know her, better than she imagined he would after so long away. She must crush these thoughts. He would be her brother-in-law and nothing more. Still, if he wished to give her away to her father to be dealt with, he would know right where to lead her father to find her. So why point him in the opposite direction?

Of course. She nodded her head, content in her assessment. He wanted her to be spared further humiliation. In that he was indeed acting just like a brother would. That is what Brian would do and had done the many times she had fled from Bevvy's scolding. The assessment drew a lump to her throat and tears stung behind her lids.

Head lowered and hands clasped, Anne turned to the forest beyond the clearing. Obviously he had come because of what she'd told him when they met. He wanted to be sure the contract for Beverly's hand would hold despite Rathmore's offer. How she regretted going to the library when she saw his carriage. Still, she wished she had heard more of the conversation and kept her mouth shut when her father confirmed his intention of be rid of her to another man intent on her sister.

Anne scrubbed her fingers against her eyelids. Always second best. She felt her lips tremble. No, not second best, simply an alternative. More as a burden to be disposed of. How would she and Beverly ever overcome this predicament?

Beverly was right after all. Anne squared her shoulders and adjusted her skirts, flicking at the dust. She mustn't be selfish and run away like a little girl.

What would Beverly do? She would start to act like the woman she wanted them to consider her to be.

Anne would not betray her sister and leave her alone to wonder at treachery. In this, finally, her sister must come first. Everything hinged on Beverly. Everyone wanted Beverly. It was high time Anne considered Beverly.

As the men could no longer be seen or heard, Anne retraced her steps, avoided the vines, scrubbed her palms along her cheeks, and returned to the house. She needed to talk to Bevvy.

Gingerly she moved through the front foyer toward the wide, spreading staircase. Beverly remained where Anne had left her moments before, though now she sat on the bottom stair, elbow on knee, palm under chin. Her smooth features were pinched in a repose so unfamiliar to her typical features, Anne paused her step and took a second glance. Beverly tapped one of her nails against her front tooth, seemingly lost in her own thoughts.

Upon hearing Anne approach, she shifted her gaze to meet Anne's and lowered her hand to her lap. There she laced her fingers and straightened her spine.

Anne tried to smile. She pressed her hands against her abdomen and pulled in a bracing breath. Her knees seemed to cease working, and she felt flat-footed, unable to move forward. What could she say? What would her sister think of her? Would she be to blame for her sister's eternal unhappiness?

Beverly's stare locked on hers. Her blue eyes pooled, leaving her eyes moist, but the threatened tears did not spill.

"Father promised you to Rathmore?" Her voice

quaked, and three fingers covered her trembling mouth.

Anne now wished she had told Bevvy all that had transpired. As she studied her sister's shattered features, she felt more ashamed than ever. She had been locked in her own misery, too consumed to consider another.

"I almost thought he would give Henry's proposal consideration." Bevvy shook her head and tried to smile. "I should have known better. Father's locked into the idea of families uniting, no matter what. It doesn't seem to matter what any of us wants. Our lives, our ambitions…" A shuddered breath escaped. "Our love. He's never cared for any of that."

"I won't do it," Anne responded, leaping forward to take her sister's ice-cold hands in her own. She dropped to her knees in front of Beverly to meet her gaze. "Do you hear me? I won't do it. I will not be the cause of your heartache."

"What are we to do? We females have no choice in these matters."

Still, Beverly's eyes rounded with hope, the blue irises so intent and clear Anne felt momentarily lost in their depths. For the first time Anne could remember, her sister seemed at a loss, their roles suddenly reversed.

Normally, Bevvy maintained constant composure. She was the one always in control. She'd taken on the role of mother, and Anne realized in that moment that perhaps she hadn't taken the time to rely upon herself as much as she should have because she always had someone else to taken on all the obligations she didn't want to face. Her big sister was always the one who had all the answers, who knew all the right next moves. Anne could always follow, knowing her sister would take care of things. How wrong she had been in her expectation of Bevvy.

With a suddenness as swift as the north wind, their roles seemed reversed. Anne knew this had been her doing. It had been she who let details slip to Garrett in a fit of rage that then sparked him to consult their father. Or confront him. Anne couldn't know the extent or context, but she could guess. Though it might be frowned upon for decorum's sake, she cursed herself again for not listening for more in the conversation between her father and Garrett. How she wished she had kept quiet long enough to hear their plan.

Anne pulled her sister into a hug. "Devil them all," Anne gusted. "We will win out. You will see."

"Anne," Beverly scolded in a more normal tone.

Anne smiled, pulled back, and kissed her sister's cheek. "Together, my dear. He is our father, and somewhere in there he must care for us. We have to show him what is in our best interest. The match for you with Henry is as advantageous—more so, really, than with Garrett."

She twisted to assume a seat next to Bevvy on the stairs. Contemplating, she chewed her lip, chafed her sister's hands, and racked her brain for a solution. They sat in weary silence until the normal household activities made Anne aware of how much time had elapsed. It could only be a matter of time before her father, perhaps with Garrett still in tow, returned.

"It was mother's last wish for me," Bevvy said in soft tones. "Perhaps I should, as father insists, honor her desire."

Anne cupped her sister's chin within her palm. "Bevvy dear, I cannot imagine our mother would want

95

anything but your happiness." Anne stroked her sister's cheek. "If she were here now, would she not find a solution? I feel sure she would see that love will out."

"We must appeal to our father's own sensibilities." Beverly nodded, her eyes starting to shine with a flicker of hope. "His match with mother was one of love."

Anne scanned the room before whispering, "Unlike his match with Harriet, which furthered the family fortune and allowed us to retain home and status."

"You knew about that?"

"I am not ignorant to what had been our plight."

"My dear, you do impress today." Bevvy smiled, nodding her head. "How you have grown up overnight. I declare, I think you are even taller."

Anne couldn't contain the grin.

Now Beverly squeezed Anne's hands, a warmth and glow rising in her face. "Perhaps he is swayed by his own more recent match," she said. "You are correct, Anne. We must find a way to remind him of his love of mother."

Anne stood, taking Beverly with her through their clasped hands. "Come now, Bevvy dear." She led the way up the stairs. "Let's retire to your room and think."

"Plot and scheme, you mean," Bevvy responded with an unnatural glint in her eyes.

Anne heard her father's boots on the slate floor as they reached the landing.

Chapter Thirteen

Knowing her father had returned and would be in a temper, Anne slid the bolt softly so they wouldn't be disturbed unexpectedly.

"Our lives are in utter ruins," Beverly said, covering her face with her hands and falling into her pillow.

Anne shook her head and bit back a comment. If they were going to achieve their end, she needed Beverly's influence and experience within the household.

"You have long since worked around Father and his tempers," she stated flatly, coming to sit on the edge of the bed. "Why should now be any different? Whenever you have wanted to plan a menu or hire staff, and he opposed, you won out."

"That was different," she said in a pouty tone, muffled by the down of the pillow.

"Nonsense."

"'Tis all my fault. I should never have begun with Henry. I recognized the attraction from my many silly novels, but yet..." She flipped onto her back, the twist of her skirt impeding her movement only marginally. "Now I know I cannot marry Garrett, though he has done nothing to deserve this mistreatment. And now that I know, I simply cannot marry without love."

The declaration caused Anne's stomach to erupt in

anxious flutters.

"I think…" Beverly turned her head toward Anne. "I think I somehow thought love to be this abstract thing. I could never understand the meaning behind those flowery words of poems. Yes, they were wonderful to read, such feeling and sincerity, but I could not understand them."

"And now you do?"

Beverly raised on her elbow and reached for Anne's wrist. "Yes, now I can see the words, my dear." Her fingers tightened around Anne's flesh. "I can feel their meaning. I understand the lengths someone would go for love. There truly are no boundaries."

"And you do not feel this for Garrett?"

Though she had always suspected there was no affection, Anne had to know to eliminate her guilt, for the words always had meaning for her. Her heart had ached for so long, she had come to expect it as a natural part of her being.

"Perhaps Brian could help." She bit her lip.

"He and Father have never seen eye to eye," Beverly countered, dropping back on the bed.

"Well, at a minimum, he'd offer gainful suggestions. An alternative, maybe." Anne shook her head. Unlikely.

"I never expected to love, you see," Beverly continued, turning her face to the side, her flushed cheek brighter from rubbing against the pillow. "Certainly not Henry. He was so awkward and a bit of a dandy."

The sisters shared a giggle.

"I never expected, but now…now…" Beverly swallowed and sat up, coughed a little, and straightened her dress. "I find I do not want to marry without love."

By contrast, Anne had never considered marriage without love. In fact, because Garrett was not an option, she had resigned herself to being a spinster. This was one of the reasons she had secretly learned about the healing arts.

As though gripping a lifeline, for that is how it seemed, Anne pulled her sister into a tight embrace, her long-held guilt finally released. She no longer had to consider her love for Garrett as the ultimate betrayal. Though he was still not within her grasp, she could at least work toward a favorable match for her sister and free herself to pursue life as a healer.

Anne pulled away so suddenly, to stand, that Beverly swayed and laid a bracing palm on the quilt, with a startled yip.

"You're so pale, my dear." Beverly leaned toward Anne and laid the back of her hand across her brow. "'Tis too much for one day. We—"

At a knock at the door, they both turned to the intrusion.

"'Tis your father." His gruff voice left them in no doubt of his mood. The door rattled against the lock. "Allow me to come in. Your sister has run off, and in light of new circumstances I need to speak to you. Immediately."

Beverly looked to Anne and laid her finger across her lips silencing any response Anne may have said to alert their father to her presence.

Anne hadn't realized their father thought she was still out. It was now well past dark.

Beverly stood and fluffed the heavy folds of her skirt and patted her hair before pulling a face, knowing she looked in tatters compared to her normal composed self.

"I require a few moments, Father." Beverly's strong voice gave no indication of the pain and tears of moments before. Anne gaped in awe at her sister's capabilities. "I will be down to the library presently."

From the other side of the heavy oak door, Anne heard their father huff. But without further comment, his heels scraped the floor as he turned, and heavy footfalls announced his retreat back down the hall. This only proved further Beverly's command. Anne was buoyed by the thought.

Beverly turned to Anne, hands folded in prayer between her bosom. "What can he mean?" Her two index fingers peaked in a steeple-fashion, and she raised these to her lips. "Do you think Garrett may have heard about Henry and severed the contract?"

Without answering her sister, Anne found her own palms meeting in prayer at her breast. "Could he? Could the contract be severed? You must…" Anne stepped toward Beverly, keeping her voice a low muffle, resisting the urge to bite her thumbnail. "You must sway him to consider what mother would have wanted for you. This is our chance, dear Bevvy. Sway him to remember the love match he made with our mother."

Beverly strode to the window and looked out. "He could claim me in breach, I suppose. Oh, my."

The thumb won out, and Anne bit the toughened skin at the edge. Oh, that she may have held both tongue and temper so she would have known the extent of the discussion. "Shall I join you?"

"Yes, darling," Beverly said, turning from the

window. "Garrett's carriage is gone, so we must face the consequences, whatever they may be."

A war-hardened general could not have approached the battleground with as much determination as her sister, Anne thought. She dropped her hands, squared her shoulders, and followed her sister to the door. Together they descended the stairs and entered the study.

Gerald turned at their approach, his face haggard. Before he could say a word, Beverly held up her palm to stall his expected tirade. "I have made up my mind. I won't do it," she said, voice only cracking slightly as she held tight to Anne's hand for support. "I will not marry Garrett McGuire."

Taking courage, Anne squeezed her sister's fingers and nodded. "And I will not marry Rathmore. Father, you cannot use me as though I am a consolation prize to be given away."

"Mother would never have approved," Beverly said. "She made the contract with love on her mind. Love for her very best of acquaintances. Love for the children we were. Love because that is what she had with you, Father."

In an uncharacteristic calm, their father opened his mouth, but then shut it again. The scowl at his brow smoothed, and his response seemed both taken aback and saddened.

While they watched, he walked the perimeter of the room where the floor-to-ceiling bookcases displayed priceless, leather-bound volumes collected by their family for generations. Though many a family treasure had been sold over the years prior to his marriage to Harriet, he'd never stooped to depleting the library.

When he came to stand facing them, he crossed his arms over his broad chest and scrutinized each of them in turn before resuming his march. Beverly squeezed her fingers and slightly shook her head, indicating they were not to break the silence.

Gerald continued to circle, and the agony of simply watching would have been too much to bear had Anne been alone. He performed this exercise for no less than three cycles. Finally, he stopped.

"McGuire is the only heir to a fortune. To give this up, even for a title, upsets the stability of the family. Your mother wished for your happiness and for this financial security. It is the finest match we could make for you, decided a decade ago when you were still children playing in the garden. It links our lands and our families." Their father puffed his cheeks. "Beverly, you will lack for nothing."

Beverly raised her pointed chin. "The Rathmores too have vast holdings and a title to match. All from more legitimate means."

Neither Anne nor their father enjoyed the implications of the words. Though it be true, the method of the elder McGuire coming into his fortune remained a hushed legend of Blackbeard's treasure. This was no longer spoken about in polite society.

Beverly seemed not to notice. "A match with Rathmore opens doors, and I would be wed for love. Certainly, we can agree, this would further appeal to mother's ultimate wish for her daughters."

"Rathmore will be a perfect match for Anne."

"No," Beverly said, and the word seemed to bounce off the walls with untold resonance. "Henry's proposal was for me. Can you—" She broke her hold with Anne and stepped toward their father. "Can you for once see what this would do to Anne? How can you possibly imagine Anne or Rathmore being successful at a match made in such a way?"

She shook her head, linking her hands at the front of her waist. "Henry's proposal was for me, and I would like to accept."

Instead of making demands, as was common for their father, he puffed his cheeks yet again and rolled back on his heels. Anne bit her lip, puzzled with his lack of temper.

After several "um-hums," whereby Anne and Beverly exchanged mystified glances, Beverly gulped a breath and continued. They were on the verge, and Anne didn't know what they could do to move their father over the precipice.

"To me, Garrett is detestable," Beverly began, her words rushed. "We are not matched. We have never gotten on, even as children, despite our mothers' best attempts. Truly, we have hardly exchanged a word since his return. For all I know, he could be running a fleet of pirates now."

"Brian is his second," their father cut in. "You call your own brother a pirate?"

Beverly smiled, a patient shift of her lips, and shook her head. "Certainly not. But you have heard the rumors as certainly as I. Unlike the Rathmores, the McGuires know no side for loyalty. They have not declared in our fight in the new world. As a wife, you would expect me to go along with this? To me, that is not the making of a fit match."

"Pah to the rumors. You speak of politics, for which you are ill equipped to offer an opinion," Gerald said, raising a hand that called an end to the discussion as Harriet entered the room. "What do we care of the rumors, when you will have more than enough money and land to outlast idle gossip."

"What's this of pirates and rumors?" Harriet asked. "The McGuires will be in attendance at the royal regatta tomorrow, and we must prepare."

Bevvy's fingers trembled. Had they lost? What more could they do?

"The supper bell will ring, and you must dress, the pair of you." Harriet fanned her fingers in dismissal. "'Tis a woman's duty to marry well. You know this already. Stop upsetting your father."

"Mother," Beverly began, titling their father's second wife in a manner Anne could never do. "I know my place. Truly I do. But I tell you now, as a woman who must know, as you do, being the second wife—"

"Hush," Harriet cut in, her cold gray eyes slicing through the sisters. "I will not side against my husband. You do not know this. The McGuires have a fleet of profitable ships. The contract has been made. We will speak no more about this. Gerald, we must prepare. We have guests arriving shortly."

The sisters left and returned to their rooms. Shortly thereafter, properly attired, Anne rejoined her sister, who sat at her dressing table. Beverly looked more determined than ever, and Anne's heart soared with expectation.

"I shall speak to Garrett myself," Beverly declared. "Obviously he knows of Henry's proposal, else he would not have spoken to Father. That Father has not demanded immediate action tells me he is wavering. You saw him. You witnessed the impact of mention for

Mother's sake. Had Harriet not come when she had...that is no never mind." She fanned her fingers. She drew an audible breath, her chin set at a resolute angle. "He and Garrett spoke, and we do not know the elements of the conversation. 'Tis foolish to guess. I shall simply ask."

Chapter Fourteen

The wind rolled up the river, blowing moist from the north, and Garrett predicted rain by the morrow. He stepped out of the carriage and reviewed the clear sky above. The sun had dawned on the cloudless horizon with the perfect amount of force to fill a sail readied for a race up the river. Now the afternoon heat penetrated his clothing, and he almost dreaded having to be out in a crowd on such a wonderful day best spent at sea.

He dismissed his driver and strode the boulevard, heels crunching in the gravel. He couldn't contain his longing to be back on the swaying decks of his own vessel rather than landlocked as he negotiated nuptials.

Was there still a discussion being had? Certainly the old man couldn't force a situation. The main point was to avoid loss of face, loss of family connection, and financial penalty. If Gerald didn't consider his revised offer, or chose to claim Garrett in breach, he would be entitled to financial compensation. Tongues would certainly wag with that tidbit. The very people who welcomed him now would turn against him, with all that his father had built through these strategic connections potentially lost.

Yet the solution seemed so simple at this point, Garrett was impatient with both the process and the waiting. Gerald's obstinance was wearing thin. Devil be damned, perhaps it was time to leave.

106

Then there was his Bessy. He couldn't wrap his head around calling her Anne. She'd never be Anne to him, and that said it all and more. Could he leave her now? Perhaps he should have left her in the box of his memories and disobeyed his father and not returned. He recalled the kiss and his need for more. He wanted her as he had never wanted anything before. Even command of his ship.

Noise of the gathering crowd drew him from his thoughts. Mackenzie had come by separate carriage, and he tried to spot him. Garrett smiled. McGuire Senior never wanted to be tied to any social engagement too long and traveled alone to be able to depart on his own schedule. It took only a moment to spot the man. As was typical, he wasn't hard to find, being the tallest in the crowd.

Then Garrett's stomach knotted at the sight of Gerald by his side, MacLeod's robust nature a jovial counterpoint to his stubborn insistence to adhere to the original agreement. That man couldn't see reason if it jumped up and slapped him, or so it seemed. Garrett hoped it didn't come to that as a resolution, for he'd made up his mind. There was no way he would marry Beverly. Not now.

Just how much had Bessy overheard? His hands dug deep into his pockets, while his father sauntered out of the crowd to meet him. Mackenzie lifted a handkerchief to his nose periodically to block the pungent odor from the streets. Had Gerald filled him in on the situation? He needed to spare his father these kinds of concerns. As current head of their financial empire, he would need to know he could depend on Garrett to take care of business, and to Mack this marriage contract was a commercial concern.

Without doubt, Mackenzie would know soon enough. But based on his smooth brow, the older man remained in the dark, and Garrett intended to keep him that way until the agreement was finalized—which was until Garrett got his own way.

Mack stowed the slip of material in his breast pocket and lifted his chin to a meandering party ahead. "That wind bag, Lord Gilbert, is regaling the ladies with stories from his travels abroad," his father announced as they strode past, striving to avoid the mass mingling at the entrance to the garden party. "More married women dance across his sheets in a season than across the polished floors at Chelsea House."

Garrett laughed openly. This is how it had always been between them. An easy understanding. He'd admired the relationship his father and his mother shared, and despite his lack of affection for the woman he had termed "the replacement," he did wish his father would find someone in his twilight years. He worried about the man being alone.

"Not widowed yet a year and already the randy old rooster. Are you pondering entering the competition for eligible ladies?" Garrett couldn't contain a snort of laughter at Mackenzie's expression. "You old rogue."

The older man sliced a glance in his direction, a mere smirk lifting his cheek. "Ah, but here…" He pointed ahead to the colorful array of fabrics swaying like a flock of exotic birds. "I see your fiancée has arrived."

Keeping to the comedy to cover his own composure, Garrett nudged the older man in his well-heeled girth. "A wonder you haven't stolen her for yourself."

"As if I would," Mack said, drawing himself taller, pulling in the slight belly which had slipped its confines. "I am a man of principle, though a fine specimen she is."

"So says the pirate."

"Puh."

To be sure, the pale pink gown complimented Beverly's fair complexion to perfection. Though, as always, whether in dirt-spattered smocks, barefoot, with temper, or in the finest of silks, it was his Bessy who held his fascination. How had it taken so long for him to recognize this? Perhaps, had he come home more often and paid attention when he did, he may have avoided this present complication.

Nothing to be done about that now. He was doing the best he could. Acknowledging a liberty of anyone in the crowd, he allowed his gaze to rake the waif from bonnet to slippered foot. The midnight-blue day gown brought a shine to her sun-kissed skin and burnt copper hair. The curls were tamed into a coiffeur. He preferred them tumbled free and as wild as the woman.

Here was one unafraid of being out of doors. He could easily compare her to the vigor of her brother, Brian, in his element on board ship. The slender skirt gave the appearance of height, despite her barely reaching to Beverly's shoulder. The roundness of her eyes seemed greater amongst the crowd. Her innocence in such gatherings made him want to draw her away to the privacy of the garden, where she would be protected from pomp and fancy.

As though sensing his scrutiny, her eyes met his

across the crowd. While he hoped for a smile, her eyes narrowed and her brow furrowed. The look on her face did not encourage confidence regarding how she had interpreted what she'd overheard in her father's library.

Turning as though with intention, Bessy linked her arm within her sister's and turned to walk down the cobbled path closer to the river. This being the first time Garrett had seen them together since his return, he was struck by their obvious fondness for one another. Somehow, he hadn't considered their affection. This perhaps caused a complication. Not for the first time, he wondered how his proposal would be received, if, in fact, Gerald even acquiesced to accept.

Gerald had come into proximity with the sway of the socialites. He tried to catch Gerald's eye as the older man went by a moment later with his wife on his arm. Harriet seemed prepared to stop, but other than a courtesy nod, the elder McGuire preceded Garrett through to the vast gardens, giving nothing away.

He hadn't time to contemplate the meaning when Beverly held out her hand to him.

Pretending no previous encounter with either of them, he removed his hat. "My dear Miss MacLeod. A vision, as always," he said as he bowed to kiss the top of her glove. Turning his gaze to Bessy, he repeated the maneuver. "Miss Anne, you light the day."

Color flooded her cheeks, and he wondered how the rest of her body would react to his attention. A stirring erupted in his loins, and he averted his gaze.

His father, more accustomed to such occasions, treated the ladies to a poetic rendition of how they enlivened any party. "You are the jewels which everyone longs to see."

Beverly smiled, her eyes crinkled, and she demurred. Bessy avoided his presence and cast her gaze beyond his father to her sister. Love shone in the mossy depths.

As his father resumed his full height, releasing Beverly's hand, she turned to Garrett. Her direct blue gaze locked with his, and his stomach turned with sudden misgiving.

Handing her sister's arm over to his father, Beverly patted Bessy's wrist, then nodded. An unspoken communication seemed to pass between them. Turning, she took his arm with grace. "You will accompany me through the garden, Garrett?"

He couldn't stop his gaze from traveling to Bessy first before nodding and patting her fingers where they lay gently on the broadcloth. "Of course."

Without being told, seeming ignorant of the undercurrent, his father followed suit, holding out a crooked elbow for Bessy.

"A word once inside," Beverly whispered, just loud enough to be heard.

Knowing it would not appear strange for the engaged couple to move off down a side path on their own, after entering the vine-covered, arched entrance, they veered off the main path by a lush apple tree heavy with fruit. The air was much sweeter within the walled confines, away from the sewer of the streets. He breathed deeply, quelling his nerves as to what to expect.

As the noise of the crowd diminished amongst the thick foliage, Beverly pulled him to a stop. For a moment he wondered if she intended a pre-marital tryst. His stomach churned with indecision. Garrett scanned

111

her face. Immediately, he understood her intention more to conversation than intimate matters. He drew out his handkerchief to mop his brow.

She appeared not to notice his discomposure. Her own anxieties could be felt through the tightness of her grip. Her arm remained laced with his and her face resembled a granite statue, a determined slant to her mouth.

"Garrett…" Her other hand swung to brace his arm, and the pressure of her fingers bit through the fabric of his day jacket. "We cannot wed. We are mismatched, have been since childhood, and I believe you see this as clearly as I."

Garrett stepped back with the unexpected bluntness of her words, which so echoed his own sentiments. Did she have the mystical ability to read minds? Of course. He nodded his head, understanding—she wanted to accept Rathmore. Still, he pulled back marginally, processing what this could mean. Used to being in control, this was not the way he expected to deal with the matter.

Sheltered by the trees, he allowed the small distance between them to grow. Beverly released her grip and placed her hands along the front of her dress, lacing her fingers, but not before he saw the tremble.

"I do not mean to hurt you, though…" She cast him a small smile. "I do not flatter that my words will impact you emotionally." Her lips quirked up on one side before she lightly licked her lips and drew an audible breath. "I understand, like you, our mothers' intention with the contract…excuse me, I babble, please forgive me. You see, I seek to explain a situation as though you were a stranger, which to me you are."

Her blue gaze roamed his face. As the pause of her words stretched, her hands flew apart and reached imploringly for him. She took a step closer. He didn't move. When she stopped, her mouth had firmed into a hard line, an unaccustomed look for such an attractive face.

"You must know I do not love thee," she said. "I firmly believe you lack the adequate affection for me. We would be embarking on a life of misery. Anne and I agree, our mothers would not have wanted this for us."

"Anne?"

"Oh." She squeezed his forearm. "Do not be concerned. Anne is not only my sister but a trusted confidante."

A faraway look glossed her eyes. "She does not know it, but my sister is my rock. She is my strength. I would not have had the courage to approach you had it not been for her." She stopped and pulled a breath as though quaking from lack of air. "You do strike the imposing form, but Anne assured me this was not the case."

Then she stepped back a pace, dropping her hands again. "I do wonder how she came to such a notion, though I see she is correct. Pray, sir, do not despair that she knows the subject of our conversation."

His mind rattled. "And what is the subject of our conversation?"

His heart seemed to hammer once, then stop, while his breath hitched. Was this a trap? But this woman, strong in her own right, did not strike him as the vain girl of her youth. In fact, if he were so inclined, had he not known Bessy as his one true match, he might well appreciate such a woman as this for a wife.

Caution made him clamp his jaw to frivolous comment. Reel out the line sparingly. Beverly appeared a fair wind, yet he'd known many a gale to ride the coat tails of a fine day's breeze. "A contract holds no emotion."

Beverly nodded once, as though she had expected this resistance, which only served to verify she knew nothing of his conversation with her father. She drew her bottom lip between small white teeth. The action reminded him of Bessy.

The silence stretched as she seemed to contemplate her next words. She nodded, released her lip, and raised her white-gloved hand. "I understand this must strike you as highly unconventional. But we are not made for one another, and I feel if we work together, we can come to mutual terms."

He bent slightly to eliminate the gap of height in the event someone may indeed be listening. Despite the largeness of the gardens and the gull-like cackling of the crowd streaming by the other side of the tree line, he would take no chances.

"You love another."

Her mouth formed a slight o and her eyes widened. She blinked several times, and he allowed the moment so she might compose herself.

"Henry—I mean, Rathmore...who told you?" Her face paled, and standing this close, he noticed a slight pink edge to her eyes as though she had been crying recently. "What will you do?"

Garrett straightened, placed his fist under his chin, and a hand under his elbow. "What do you want to do?"

"Marry Henry." The words whooshed from her lips.

114

Garrett forced himself not to step back. His jaw had slackened and would have fallen open if not for his hand beneath. Beverly was not trying to catch him out or trap him in any way. Could they work together to achieve mutual ends? Here they were working at common purpose, but individually. They would stand a better chance at success working together. This he understood from his own crew. At cross purposes, even trying to assume the same end, they would take longer and often fail. Working together, they would have sure triumph.

He tapped a finger against the cleft of his chin. He needed to know how much she knew. Surely if the sisters were as close as they seemed, Bessy would have confided their father's intentions as well, revealed his discussion. Yet Beverly appeared ignorant.

"But is Anne not promised to our fine duke?" He almost choked on the words, wanting to drive his fist into any other man laying a claim to his Bessy.

Beverly opened and closed her mouth, then turned from him. "H-How…how do you know that?" Arms crossed over her chest, she strode to the rose bush, then back.

"Father told you," she said, halting her steps in front of him and pointing her finger. "He had no right. She will not accept."

"She has a choice?"

"You do not know her as I do," Beverly countered. "She is strong willed. She—"

Her fingers covered her lips stifling any further flow of words.

"Your face, Garrett." She reached to lay a gloved palm along his cheek. "What have I missed? You have

115

your own affection tied elsewhere."

It was time to draw an end to the cat-and-mouse game. If he wanted his plan to work, Beverly was providing every opportunity for him to achieve his end.

"I love her."

Chapter Fifteen

Anne could not stay away. As soon as she could, she followed to the garden. She must know of Beverly's success...or defeat.

Catching movement from the corner of her vision, Anne pretended not to notice and stepped to the side. Glancing over her shoulder, she saw Harriet flap her fingers, bidding Anne to join the matrons' group. She couldn't evade.

"Anne, dear," Harriet intoned, a little too loudly, so surrounding peers would hear her as well. A certain slight aroma heralded her early indulgence in the abundant spirits present at the festivities. "I saw Beverly walk off with our Mister McGuire. A ship's captain of one of the family's vessels, don't you know. Wealthy beyond measure." The older woman nodded significantly and raised her chin to the other ladies present. "His father did right to send him off to the navy at fourteen. Earned his commission, so I'm told. Left as a first lieutenant, no less. Now a captain of their own fleet of merchant vessels."

Anne laced her fingers and waited while appropriate ohs and ahs exhausted to mild murmurs. Then Harriet again turned to Anne. "Go and find the young couple. If we do not refresh soon, we shall miss the races," she said with a dismissive twist of her gaze. "I want to be at the finish. How I hate going home as

117

though I bathed in the city ditches, such is the amount of dust after so much foot traffic."

Anne resisted the urge to curl her lip with the vapor emitted by her stepmother, who'd indulged in the claret and the gossip a little too early in the day. Fortunately, no one had formed a habit of paying Anne too much attention, else they may have seen the effect on her face of how her stomach knotted in ropes of anxiety. Glad of the excuse to find her sister, Anne straightened and wandered off.

Harriet's high-pitched words replayed. Anne stumbled on one of the paving stones, catching a nearby snicker at her lack of grace. If the gossips began to buzz about Garrett and Beverly, severing the contract might be an impossibility, given the scandal that would result. How would they ever pull it off? And what if the severing of one contract would hamper Bevvy's ability to proceed to an agreement with Rathmore, despite his willingness?

Anne made to pick up her skirt before treading further, then felt steadying fingers brace her elbow. She looked up, half hoping to meet Garrett's dark blue gaze.

Henry smiled. "Watch your step, Miss Anne," he said. "You wouldn't want to take a tumble in this crowd and feed the chinwags."

At a loss for a pithy response, she could only nod. Though he didn't look upon her in the same besotted fashion he showered on Bevvy, Anne could easily discern his attempt to build something from nothing. How she longed to reassure him that they were scheming to ensure he need not have to try but could be free to love her sister as Beverly loved him.

He lifted his chin. Thin lines etched downward

from his mouth, which Anne imagined as sadness to the tragedy of his love affair with Bevvy. Anne wondered if he'd heard Harriet's words. They echoed through the spaces of her brain and seemed to hang heavy in the air all around.

Anne gazed around the crowd but saw no one. "'Tis the right crowd for it," she managed at last and did her best to return the smile. Uncomfortable with his touch, she drew her elbow away from his fingers. "I must away to fetch my sister."

His brows arched, and his face seemed to take on a hopeful expression. "She is here, then?"

"Yes, and I must make haste to locate her before the regatta begins."

He crooked his arm gallantly. "Allow me to accompany you."

She almost jumped back in fright and managed to bump into a rotund woman in a voluptuous gown at least a decade out of style.

"Please excuse me," Anne stammered to both Henry and the woman, who shot a frozen stare, followed by a harrumph to her companions on the disrespect of youth these days. She moved into the crowd as quickly as she could to escape being followed by a bewildered Henry.

Casting a glance over her shoulder, Anne managed to return to the spot on the path where she had last seen Beverly leading Garrett. Would that Beverly had been successful, she prayed, gnashing at her fingers until the joints popped. They had plotted throughout the night, but in the light of day their strategy appeared feeble, at best.

While the moon etched the hours, they surmised

that the collective parentage could do little to insist on a marriage should both bride and groom protest. What seemed so logical at the time now screamed nonsensical under the rays of a dazzling sun. For where the MacLeods were property owners, the McGuires had wealth. This was all her father coveted, knowing full well that without an influx of money, despite his marriage to Harriet, the land would be lost within a generation.

Harriet's insinuation prior to an "official" announcement bounced into Anne's mind again and screamed of further sabotage to their fledging plan. If timing were everything, Anne felt sure, she and Beverly were running short.

Anne straightened her shoulders and moved off the main path to take the circuitous route toward the pond. A wall of tall aspen separated the main park, amass in people, from the more secluded gardens designed like leaves from the main trunk of a tree. Though still loud, the noise faded, as did the sour vinegar scents of too many people in close proximity. Here, the earthy aromas of growing vines and budding flowers eased the acid which threatened to upend the meager contents of her stomach. This was Anne's paradise.

The purple lilac beckoned her forward, and for the first time in what seemed like hours her chest lightened enough to breath. Folding her hands across her heart, she mouthed a silent prayer for answers. Skimming a hand across her hair to tuck wayward pieces back into place, she moved through a narrow line of cherry trees. On another day, she might have stopped to admire their blossoms, a spectacular array of pinks and white mixed with cream.

Glancing around, she was surprised more lovers hadn't taken advantage of the seclusion. Insulated from the crowds, Anne was assured she was alone. Where would they have wandered? Garrett and Beverly could be anywhere along the many paths worming this way and that. Her hands fell to her hips at a momentary loss of which direction. A horn sounded in the distance; time was running out. The racing schooners had assembled.

Almost at a loss, she listened, finally identifying Garrett's resonating tenor. She followed the sound. She couldn't discern his words, but promisingly, the tone sounded hardly angry, and Anne's heart fluttered.

Then Beverly's voice drew her up short. Anne approached with caution, not wanting to interfere. She kept her step light and soundless, the body of the foliage perfect camouflage for her presence.

"You know this for certain?" Beverly asked.

Anne edged closer; the rough trunk of the tree scraped against her forearm.

"I had our lawyer, Watkins, confer specifically," Garrett answered.

"How?"

The silence stretched. Anne resisted biting her thumbnail. Beverly's question hung heavy in the air. Anne ached to be able to see their expressions and understand more fully to what they referred. Had they reached a pact? She placed her forehead against the bark to prevent looking around and being seen and ousted for eavesdropping.

"Okay," Beverly said, her tone questioning. "But I've never heard of a proxy bride."

Anne couldn't hold her curiosity any longer. She

edged around the tree, intrigued by the turn of phrase. She too had never heard of such a thing. She moved cautiously, aware even of leaves under foot. As someone used to following the deer through the groves, she managed to keep the noise to a minimum. From this vantage point, slightly uphill from the couple, Bevvy's face could be seen in shadowed profile. She could not see Garrett, but she knew from his voice where he stood.

"That's the legal term we could stand on, yes," he said at last, pacing into Anne's sight before he disappeared again, only to re-emerge. "But she could not be a proxy for you, meaning you and I would not be wed."

Anne ached to be better informed to the "she" they referenced. She didn't understand the word "proxy." This was obviously important to their plan. Beverly sounded both pleased and hopeful. If they were speaking like this, surely this meant Garrett had agreed. Anne's heart rejoiced to imagine Bevvy happily wed to Henry, her heart's desire.

"You would be legally wed to Anne then, as we agree," Beverly said.

Anne's breath hitched.

"So what you are saying is the terms of the contract would be upheld because I was never named personally in the contract," Beverly continued. "The contract vaguely references only the daughter of…"

As if engulfed by a verbal tidal wave, Beverly's words muted in Anne's hearing while she covered her ears with her trembling hands. Anne was the "she" they referenced. Another stand in. The implications shot through Anne like a bullet, and she clamped her hands across her mouth to stem the gasp. Her ears began to ring. How could this be? Why would Beverly agree to such a thing? The point was to sever the contract, not fulfill it with a different person.

"As you've no wish to fulfill the contract, and we agree it is a legal document which does not name you specifically, then yes, Anne could be my legal wife."

"And I would be free to accept Henry."

"As you wish," Garrett agreed, coming back into view, his broad shoulders blocking Beverly's face from Anne as Beverly continued, "Then everyone gets what they want. Our fathers fulfill the union of the families. I am free. And Anne will be your wife."

A shudder passed through Anne, and she felt faint. A tingle behind her knees threatened, but she would not collapse in front of them. The traitors!

The crunch of dry grass and the breaking of a branch punctuated the silence. Anne grasped the small trunk of a tree to keep from falling. Surely even Beverly didn't know her secret heart, and that she didn't know and would barter her away opened a wound Anne had never known. Would she forever be a tool of barter? A woman of no consequence? Someone considered a "proxy"—whatever that meant?

That she longed to be Garrett's wife meant little to the arrangement, with the knowledge that he hadn't chosen her. Evidently, he was resigned to a contract of terms as a business proposal. He seemed to care little who filled the contract. That was proven when he kissed her in the woods while being promised to her sister. As a man of many ports, he was likely one of those who took the affections of women for granted.

Anne raised a hand to her brow now wet with

perspiration. Her own sister bartering her away easily, callously, without discussion—Beverly seemed no different than their father.

"Will she agree?" Garrett asked.

"She will," Beverly replied, conviction ringing in her voice. "She loves me and wants me happy in love. She will do it."

"Enough to sacrifice her own happiness and choice in love?"

Anne could listen no more. She backed away and retraced her steps in automation, drawn by the growing noise of the crowds. Escape. There must be an escape. She must find it immediately. She would find her father and make her case that she was too ill to remain.

Finding Harriet had returned to her father's side, a slight sway in her stance, Anne told her she could locate neither Beverly nor Garrett.

Harriet glanced toward the garden. "How strange," she said. "I must find them before the regatta begins. We wouldn't want people to chatter before the official nuptials are announced."

"No, certainly, my dear," Gerald agreed. "You are correct. I will remain here with Anne until you return."

Anne waited until Harriet was swallowed by the crowd. "I am ill, Father, and I must go," she announced without further preamble to her father.

He looked about to protest, then surveyed her head to toe, seeming to take in her appearance for once. He nodded and agreed with a sigh. "You will need an escort."

So relieved, she squeezed his hands. The rarity of the touch seemed to infect her father like a shock, and his eyes widened.

In response, Anne said, "Yes, please, right away. The carriage will do."

As she turned to descend the stairs, fighting a faint, Garrett's tall form appeared in her path. He looked from Gerald to her. "May I have the honor of escort?" He searched her face. "I will see she is well tended, and you need not miss the festivities."

Chapter Sixteen

As Garrett and Beverly approached the party, they came across Harriet first. In animated fashion, she engaged with a group of matrons. When she spotted them, she smiled slyly with an expression such as one might imagine representative of the many realms of Dante's Inferno.

"I was looking for you. You must have been well hidden," Harriet said. The older woman stepped away from the group and closed the distance between them. "Anne returned saying she couldn't find you."

At that moment, just across the patio, the pair saw Anne, looking desperate, and her father. Beverly stiffened at his side, and his stomach dropped. He glanced down at Beverly, whose face had turned ashen. Tucking her hand in the crook of his arm, he moved toward Gerald.

"What if she overheard?" Beverly asked.

He patted her fingers lightly. "Then we will alter our plan."

"How?"

He didn't answer as they drew near enough to overhear Anne tell her father she must leave immediately. Beverly released her grip and nodded, lifting her chin. Her gaze and raised brows indicated he must be the escort.

She dropped her grasp and stepped away before

126

being seen by her sister. "Given our plan, better it to be just the two of you. I will meet her at home."

Garrett nodded and watched her melt away into a group of her peers. He offered his assistance, striving to keep his face impassive despite the fact that Anne looked as though she wished to refuse him his offer to escort her home. Even in her temper, he had never seen her face look so disturbed.

Her stormy glare made him feel as inadequate as the junior seaman he'd once been when his father sent him into His Majesty's navy at fourteen, to make him a man. Straight white teeth gripped her lower lip. Then she turned back to her father. "No need. The coachman will suffice."

Garrett couldn't let the opportunity pass. "'Tis no trouble, I assure you."

She glanced around the crowd. He assumed she sought to find Beverly in the throng. Obviously not finding her target, her angry glare returned to him. There was a slight wobble to her lower lip. "Oh, but it is," she countered. Her tiny fist clamped against her hip and her chin jutted.

"So very kind of you, McGuire," Gerald said, a hand to Anne's back, pushing her gently toward him. "Certainly, I will rest easier knowing she is seen safely through this varied crowd of spectators. I can assume you will return promptly."

Garrett nodded. "'Twill be my pleasure."

Unable to refuse him further without a scene, Anne blinked several times, regripping her lower lip with those straight white teeth. He couldn't help the sudden image of her pulling at his own lip in that way. But now was not the time to indulge such fantasies when the muscle of her jaw worked to great effect, showing her agitation.

She scanned him from head to foot; then she nodded once. Turning stiffly, she preceded him to the path leading to the main road along the river. The regatta had not yet begun, though the colorful flags fluttered in the breeze.

Garrett lengthened his stride to keep pace. He marveled at Anne's straight back. She could have been seven feet tall the way she parted the crowd. He swallowed back a grin. This was not a time to be amused.

Based on her reaction, Garrett was left with little doubt she had indeed heard at least some of his conversation with her sister. Try as he might, he could hardly remember most of what he and Beverly had discussed. He'd been elated by her questions, her proposal, their agreement. Everything he wanted was now within his grasp, yet the woman who would be his wife had yet to consent. Based on this behavior, he didn't like his prospects. His recollection, sketchy though it was, convinced him part or portions or the conversation between himself and her sister could easily be misconstrued and taken out of the intended context if Anne had overheard.

Damn. He floundered over the best approach. Even broaching the subject seemed impossible, based on the anger emanating from her every fiber. Still, he was as happy as a man could be walking beside the woman he loved. That she might be an unwilling bride…

"An ache of the stomach, is it?" He ventured to cover the silence, nodding to people as they passed.

She shot him a glare, then returned her gaze to the

128

road ahead. The carriage was but moments away. Reaching the door, she gripped the handle and turned to him. "Really, there is no need. I will be fine from here."

"I promised your father to escort you home. I am a man of my word."

"Are you, then?"

"Yes."

She shook her head, and her palm rubbed her brow. Her fingers trailed to her lips. Two fingers paused before she folded them into a fist. "And have you given your word to my sister as well?"

A lock of hair had come loose over her ear. He reached to tuck it back.

She moved to ward off his touch and held up a palm.

Reluctantly, he dropped his hand. "Yes, I have," he replied, recalling their tentative plan. Despite Beverly's assurance, Anne did not look at all open to any suggestion of an alliance with him.

"Then you should be with her." With that, she jumped up the steps, into the coach, and closed the door behind her. Using the walking stick by the door, she thumped the roof. "Go."

Shouts erupted from within the meandering spectators. As the coachman made to maneuver the horses, a boy waved the coachman to a halt before he cracked the whip.

"'Tis the Lady Beverly, miss," the youth said, running up to them, heaving, out of breath. He pulled on Garrett's sleeve, large eyes watery. "She must come at once, sir. The lady has fainted dead away, and the master says Lady Anne must come with haste."

Anne's fingers had been gripping the open window

ledge, and she opened the door with a bang on the last of the words. Before Garrett had an opportunity to utter a word, let alone press for more information, she had moved to the lad's side and away.

Quickly, Garrett caught up with the rushing pair as Anne asked the matter.

"Dunno, really," the boy replied, his Hampton accent more pronounced with apparent growing anxiety. "The master has sent for the doctor at once, and I was away to you as he said your godforsaken— please excuse, miss. Those are his words—obsession with the herbs may assist."

Anne glanced at Garrett. "Yes. Yes, of course. If only I had my basket," she lamented, keeping pace easily with the lad. "Have you any idea?"

"We encounter a great many things at sea, but until I can see for myself…" They were rounding the bend where the gardens spread away from the waterfront. "Is she prone to fainting, then?"

"Bevvy? No, never."

The affection and worry in her tone illustrated how easily she had dropped the anger of moments before. Perhaps Beverly had been right, and she could convince Anne to this course of action after all. He picked up the pace and sprinted ahead of the youngster. He prayed nothing serious had occurred.

He glanced to his right and noted Anne directly at his side. "You are right. 'Tis no time to dally in discussion." She huffed for breath. "I know not even what I may need."

Moved away from the spectacle of the regatta to that of a tragedy, the crowd circled. Anne parted the mob quickly, moving between the spectators, her palms outstretched as though swimming a rough current. "Beverly would hate this," she muttered so only he could hear. Then, she rushed to her sister's side and dropped to her knees.

Even from a distance, Beverly appeared as white as parchment. Anne laid a hand on her sister's chest and bent to listen for breath. Garrett had seen the ship surgeon do the like on board the *Isle Sky*. Beverly's brow glistened, moist with a sheen of sweat.

Anne straightened to look to one of Beverly's companions. "Tell me what happened."

"I know not," the girl cried, fluttering her fan in agitation. "One moment she admired the aroma of the beautiful roses slipped into her hand. We marveled on who had been the secret admirer, assuming it to be you, McGuire." The young woman turned her gaze on him. "But you were nowhere about, and then the Lady Beverly fell, gasping."

Anne nodded, her nimble fingers loosening the constricting lace at her sister's throat.

"'Tis too awful," the girl muttered, turning into the arms of a companion. "Too awful by half. I cannot bear it."

"Then don't," Garrett barked, which cleared the area somewhat. Gasping at his apparent social misstep, the unquestioning sea of people dissipated a little. He knelt down for a better view. A red welt punctuated the slender collarbone, the vivid splotch rimmed with white.

"A sting," Garrett said, tenderly touching the swollen patch, which held its form.

Anne turned and gaped at him.

"A sting," he repeated, feeling around Beverly's

windpipe. "A wasp or a bee. I've seen it before, men reacting to the stinger."

Anne nodded. "I've heard of this." Her fingers skimmed along her sister's neck. She gasped. "Yes," she said, as her fingers paused their exploration. "Here." She indicated the dark center, a purple dot in the nodule on Beverly's pale skin where the shoulder crooked toward the slender neck. "A bee, I think."

"Can you grasp the end of the stinger?"

"Just," she said, pinching her fingers together.

"Careful not to allow more of the poison," he cautioned. "You need the full stinger removed."

"I have it." She held it out to him.

"What now?"

"Get her in the house." Her father stepped to her side, arms crossed over his chest. "Out of the flapping jaws of the crowd. Get her out of here. There is no need for a scene."

Anne ignored her father and turned to Garrett. "Mud first, then get her into the house. I know what we need."

Garrett leapt from the veranda to the nearest flowerbed. Using both hands, he dug down to reach the earth still moist from the morning mist. He formed it into a ball and returned to Anne's side.

She nodded and molded the clay around the wound.

"We need a poultice to draw the poison," he said, scooping an arm under Beverly's head. "She's barely breathing."

"I'll take her," a voice from the side said. Henry stepped forward and gathered Beverly into his arms. "Will she be okay?"

"Of course," Anne said, turning to Garrett but addressing both men. "Have you any lavender?"

Henry shook his head, gathering Beverly into his arms.

Anne pointed at Garrett. "Then find some. We will need apply one drop only."

"And honey," Garrett added.

"Yes, honey," she concurred. "We've no time. I must into the garden for a poultice. Moss and plantain."

Garrett was reaching for Anne's hand when he was stopped by the high-pitched tones of Anne's stepmother. "This is most unseemly," Harriet said, her voice drowning out the others. "What is this commotion?"

"Do be quiet," Gerald hissed as Garrett took Anne's hand in his and left the startled onlookers. This day would be the fodder of discussion behind the fans aflutter for quite a time.

Anne ran at his side and then pulled him up short as she pulled both slippers and stockings from her feet, leaving them where they fell as they rushed on.

The burble of the river beckoned. "Had your man lived, then?" She puffed as they neared their destination.

"What?"

"Your man on board," she repeated. "Had he lived?"

He shook his head and moved to the water's edge. There she pulled a large rock loose of the bank, heedless of the muck and water staining her gown. "Underneath," she instructed, showing him what she wanted.

"Yes," he replied. "This is what the surgeon used."

Taking damp handfuls, she made a pouch in her gown, dumped in a large quantity, stood, took Garrett's hand, and made to run back.

Chapter Seventeen

Anne drew great gulps of air, blinking rapidly to clear her vision. Sweat had started to run from her forehead and drip into her eyes. She swallowed once, then twice, and still the great lump in her throat would not be dislodged. *Not her Bevvy.* Trembling fingers swiped across Beverly's cheek. Thank God she hadn't given in to tears. She'd be no use at all if she gave in to panic.

From across the room, she eyed the contents of her medical bag, laid as she had left them. Instead of any personal items, her healing supplies decorated the dresser table. Only now, with Bevvy safe at home, both of them ensconced in her bedroom on the third floor of the manor house, could Anne allow some fear a vent. Safe, but in a weakened state, her sister lay in the bed, finally breathing easily and regularly. Alive.

Anne cupped her cheeks with her palms, smoothing skin against skin until she drew the knuckle of her index finger into her mouth. How close they'd come to losing her. Too close.

She hated to think what might have happened had she already left. If she hadn't had Garrett by her side giving command to her instruction.

No, she couldn't delve down that path of thinking.

She stood by the bed. Her sister looked so small. Fragile even.

Beverly had been a force in Anne's life from the time of her earliest memories. It was hard to reconcile this delicate, venerable creature to the vivacious Beverly. Had she always been this tiny and Anne simply didn't notice, assuming her a giant to her own diminutive stature?

Anne walked to the wash basin to rinse and wring out the cloth. Returning to the bed, she laid the back of her hand against Bevvy's brow, confirming no fever. She gently dabbed the soft material over Bevvy's cheeks. Though her color remained high, the peach of her complexion showed. Purple smudges circled the closed lids, and the cascade of lashes fanned out, no longer twitching in agitation.

Riled by the continued tremble of her fingers, she pulled her arm back, fisted and flexed her fingers. She had stood so fast her back snapped. Unexpectedly, that had felt good. She glanced at her sister, then turned to the window. Shaken to the core at her near loss, she felt ashamed of her recent anger. How awful life would have been if the last memory she'd had were of being incensed by something she hadn't even bothered to ask Bevvy about but simply assumed the worse.

Contrite, Anne returned to the giant four-poster bed and fell to her knees. She kissed the pale cheek. "Forgive me," she whispered, fitting Bevvy's hand within her own. "'Twill be okay now."

Tears again stung behind her lids, and her throat thickened. She could not release this torrent. She glanced to the cracked ceiling and blinked them away. Still the blue tinge which had so recently framed her sister's nose and mouth haunted as a framed image behind her eyes.

Through the doorway of her mind, she again watched Beverly gasping to breathe, eyes bulged, pupils so dilated as to appear like black orbs. All the while she clung to Henry's hand. She had tried to speak several times, but the words were lost in the swelling of her neck. She grabbed Anne's wrist and seemed to scream without sound. Her fingers dug into Anne's flesh, bruising while she writhed in panic.

Anne rubbed her wrist now, wearing the bruise like a badge. Just then Beverly's eyes flicked open, drawing Anne away from her dark thoughts. Her sister's lips lifted, though she seemed to lack the energy to form a smile.

Anne laid a palm against her velvet cheek. "Lie still," Anne cooed. "You're okay,. my dear."

"Anne, dear." Her sister's voice rang as a hoarse whisper, stretched as though it had lacked use and traveled a great distance to emerge. Anne leaned in, considering it a gift from the angels and just as sweet in context. "What happened?"

Anne made to speak, but the words stuck. She smiled, tilted her head, swallowed, and tried again. The storm would break. In the clear gaze from her sister's shimmering eyes, she could be strong no more. Tears rolled freely where her voice still failed.

"That dreadful, then," Bevvy said, turning her face to the pillow. "I shall never be allowed in public again."

Anne lifted Beverly's hand to her lips. She shook her head.

"Oh, but your pale face, your tears, your disappointment in me, does tell me all I cannot remember." Beverly rolled her head on the pillow. "I recall the beautiful flowers. The bee nestled in the bud startled me. I believe it was my cry which caused the bug to abandon his occupation…then the—" She raised a hand to her neck. Her words had gained strength with the use of her voice. "The sting. How it pained! Even now the site throbs. Oh dear…how I hate the antics of those who faint. I am sure not even my Henry will look upon me now. Was it such a scene? Poor Garrett, how much he has had to put up with."

Anne swiped her tears, blew her nose, and coughed to dislodge the lump in her throat. "Certainly not," she said, finding her voice at last to reassure her sister that no one could have done a faint with more graceful justice. "Your Henry will be ever more in love with you. And that Garrett—puh, what do you care? You are never to fear, my darling. You were brave and need only be concerned that you are well."

Beverly's eyes grew moist. "My Henry. Anne, could this be true? Has Garrett convinced our father? Will he allow the match?" Beverly returned her gaze to Anne's. The blue depths held a pleading.

Anne longed to ask about the scheme, but she didn't want to ruin the moment. Instead, she pretended ignorance. Time enough to work through these issues later. "Perhaps after almost losing you he will reconsider this unreasonable stoicism," Anne said.

Beverly squeezed Anne's fingers. Anne wiped the moisture away and smiled, reassured when Bevvy's face assumed a tranquil appearance. Soon the eyes fluttered shut while her breathing drew in, then out, with regular relaxed motion.

Anne wished the tension in her own shoulders would dissipate, but she knew not her place in the world now. She would plan and make her own way.

Confusion muddled her thoughts and churned like acid in her stomach. If she were to be a wife, quite certainly it would be to one man or another who didn't want her. What then? The convent? There, at least she might be allowed to practice her healing.

As she lifted the cloth from Beverly's brow, she was exhausted by the consideration. What did it matter now? Bevvy was safe. Anne turned her face to glance out the window to a cloudless sky. Fresh hope bloomed. If she could have a hand in securing Beverly's happiness, she would agree to whatever her sister and Garrett proposed. She would listen. Even if she were second choice, she'd be married to a man she loved. That would have to be enough. Perhaps in time Garrett might come to share some affection.

Moments passed in silence. The house around them creaked and settled, then resettled, as old houses do. In the distance, indistinct voices murmured, and Anne knew she should relate Beverly's improved state to the rest of the family. Father would summon her shortly, and her sister seemed to be growing stronger moment by moment before her very eyes, like a flower opening its petals to the sun's warmth. Bevvy's color had lost the fevered purple sheen.

As Anne sat beside the bed watching Bevvy sleep, she pondered what their loves might be after this moment. When at last Bevvy opened her beautiful cornflower-blue eyes, Anne could contain herself no longer. After getting her sister some water, she asked, "What did you and Garrett agree?"

"Oh, Anne, my darling dear sister, what did you hear?"

Anne dropped her gaze. "Enough."

139

Beverly's gaze drifted to the window, then back. Unshed tears pooled before she blinked them away. "Would that you had not overheard, and I could have discussed these options with you first."

"But we had agreed before—"

Beverly's slender fingers wrapped around Anne's narrow wrist. "Oh, my dear," she said looking at the red-and-purple bruise. "Did I do that?" Her thumb ran along the discoloration.

Anne patted her hand and the linked fingers. "'Tis nothing. Go on, please. I need to know."

"Yes," she said and squeezed to emphasize the word. "You are right. You need to know, and as we intended. We did have a plan, you and I, we did. But as Garrett and I talked…for the first time, Anne, we talked about a future everyone else had planned out for the two of us without ever consulting us."

Beverly released her grip as though suddenly exhausted. "I always blamed him, you see," Beverly continued, her voice strong but weary, resigned. "As though he had been involved in this fiasco of marriage and family union. To my way of thinking, Garrett held me back from making my own choice. Held me back from Henry."

Anne stayed by the bedside, afraid to move and disrupt her sister's contemplation.

"Even as children he and I were thrown together, but I would always go off on my own and leave the three of you." Beverly ran a hand over her face and through her hair, which lay matted around her head like a halo. "What a dreadful mess I am, dear Anne."

"Please continue," Anne said, her voice almost pleading. They could deal with her sister's vanity later.

"In the garden, with no walls between us, I saw him as a man in the same position as I. Perhaps even more imprisoned, in fact, for he is expected to give up his ship and a life of adventure he clearly loves. I saw that this proposal offered as much of an imposition to him as it does to me, and perhaps..." Her words trailed as the sound of voices passed in the hallway.

Anne's heart raced, expecting an intrusion. When they—likely the servants—passed the door without knocking, she released the breath she'd been holding.

"Would it be so very bad?" Beverly asked, taking Anne's hand in her cool grip. "As children you seemed to always want to be around him and Brian. You were one of them. Always game for the adventure. Do you think you could learn to love Garrett as a husband? Would it be so terrible a match?"

Anne quaked. Here was her every dream being laid out for her. Only her pride held her back. Was she so old-fashioned as to want a husband who wanted her? "But to be second best."

Anne hated the sound of her own voice as she said the words, churlish and petulant, as though she were the only one in the world to agree to an arranged union. The very fabric of the society in which they were meshed had been fashioned by contractual matches based on lineage and business succession, arrangements made for the parties.

"Only to you, Bevvy, could I confide, that like you I did secretly hope to be a bride one day chosen, as Henry has asked for your hand and you so want to be married to him. Not someone foisted upon my groom and not even first choice of the contract."

"Oh, Anne, my dearest. How awful and selfish you

must imagine me."

Despite her worry, now that the worst seemed over, some of her anger returned despite her previous promise to let the wrath go. "How could you, Bevvy," she wailed in a strangled whisper, completely undone by her sister's betrayal. "We had agreed to have the contract terminated. Not to have me substitute, be some sort of—what did you call it?—proxy bride. That is no better than what Father proposed to Rathmore. No different at all, save the fact that you want Henry and not Garrett."

"It wasn't like that." Beverly struggled to sit up in bed. She fought with the accumulated pillows until Anne reached down to assist.

"I heard it with my own ears."

Beverly huffed and found her spot, clearly wearied by the exertion. "Then you heard not all of it and not enough."

"Yes, enough," Anne countered. "Oh, do be careful. Perhaps we can talk about this later when you are stronger."

"I am strong enough now."

Anne shook her head. "So I am to be the proxy for you—"

"No, Anne." Beverly shook her head so violently her hair flew about her face. "He loves you and only you. He wants only you. He told me. It is you, my dear."

Anne slumped back. Her hand flew to her throat. Of all the things Beverly could have said, this was the very last Anne expected.

"It cannot be true."

Beverly's outstretched hand caressed Anne's

cheek. "To be fair, I don't think he even knew until he saw you again at the ball," Bevvy continued, easing a loosened strand of hair behind Anne's ear. "I pretended not to have seen him at the ball. That was Father's big surprise, after all." She smiled, and Anne realized how strong her voice had grown in the last moments. "Really, how could I have possibly missed the dashing Captain Garrett McGuire, home from his grand adventures at sea. The rumor mill was a-buzz—"

"I didn't hear a thing," Anne confessed.

"Of course not, Anne dear." Beverly smiled in acknowledgment. "You timid thing. You were more concerned about keeping your balance on those heeled slippers and scared to death of what to say if anyone dared to make conversation. Oh, it is all our fault for putting you in such a ghastly position."

"But I spoke to people," Anne protested.

"Matrons, dear." Beverly nodded her head and cupped her cheek before dropping her arm back to the blanket. "What do they know about dash and adventure?"

Anne screwed her face up in memory, trying to recall that dreadful evening. "Henry?" Beverly had instructed her to dance with Henry.

"Oh yes, my Henry," Beverly said. "He'd never mention another rival, let alone one that he knew shared a history with me."

"Did he not know about the contract?"

"My God, no." Beverly's bowtie lips pulled flat. "It was this which spurred me on at that ball. After my dance with Henry, I went to see Father, and that's when I saw Garrett. Fortunately, he had his back to me, helping you with your shoe."

Anne felt a flush rise to her cheeks at the memory, now tender in recall. "You are a cheeky actress. Helping a woman with her shoe does not mean love." Anne shot her sister an accusing stare. Dare she wish?

Beverly shrugged the comment aside. "I watched him with you and remembered when we were children. The time you were nearly mauled by that mangy village dog who frothed at the mouth, and how Garrett wrestled the dog away. Oh, how you made him sound like a great Viking warrior!"

"And you made fun, suggesting I had encouraged the dog, assuming him friendly."

"I am not a perfect sister," Beverly said. "You were always off in the wild and did have enough cuts and bruises for me to be concerned."

Anne huffed and crossed her arms over her chest, lost in the memory, feeling the scrapes as though they were fresh from today. Could it be true? Could Garrett have the same feelings for her that she had harbored for him all these years? *Impossible*, her mind shouted against the mountain fire of hope suddenly ablaze in her heart.

"Then remember," Beverly continued. "He built the tree house."

Anne shook her head, unwilling to open certain hurt. "But—"

"'Twas his suggestion, dear Anne, to alter the contract. Not mine." Beverly laced her fingers in her lap and stared down while weaving them in and out of alignment. "Truth be told, he had already had the contract altered, and that is what he came to see Father about the other day."

"How?"

Beverly shrugged. "The contract references the daughter, not me by name. According to the law, Garrett says either of us could fulfil the contract."

"But Mother's wish?"

"I love another. Henry is for me. You and I both agree she would want that." She paused to admire the many floral arrangements along the wall. "Ah." She lifted her chin to greet the arrangements as though they had been expected, now that she noticed and recognized their origin. "From Henry's mother's hothouse."

Anne nodded and turned to admire the beauties. Heat had taken hold of her whole body, and she felt the vibrations of her nerves cascade. "Father's rejection did not daunt his adoration."

"You know he calls you his Bessy. Says he will never call you Anne."

Anne smiled. She could never imagine him calling her anything but Bessy. It suited her fine.

"Tell me you can love Garrett, my dear Anne." Beverly turned an intense stare on her. Her clear cornflower gaze bore into Anne, seeking answers. "Or else I will walk away from Henry and honor the contract. I will not see you unhappy. After today, I know what I can and cannot live without, and you, my dear heart, are something I will not sacrifice...even for Henry."

Tears spilled down Anne's cheeks, unprovoked and unbidden. "But do you think me the most horrible of sisters if I could love and then marry a man so long promised to you?"

Beverly laughed then, first a willowy sound which grew in strength until tears rolled down her face and she clutched Anne to her side. The tension in the room broke with the merriment of cascading sound. "He was never mine," she wheezed. "We were but infants when our parents—our mothers, really, contrived the contract based on their friendship. You are the bride for him. You are the one he wants."

Chapter Eighteen

The great commotion of getting Beverly home had been replaced by the click of a heavy door, then deep silence. Garrett had never been good at waiting. He was a doer, and this waiting, not knowing how she was, oppressed him like the shattering weight of an ocean on a sunken ship.

As people dispersed to their duties, the mansion took on a muted quiet without solitude. Although left alone in the great room, Garrett felt the tension building not only within him, but also for the inhabitants of the house in general. Perhaps a reflection of his own state of mind, yet it seemed anxiety oozed out of the very fabric and material within the place. Despite the high ceilings and expansive setting, claustrophobia began to close in.

He paced, picking up one article, then another, perused a book left on the side table, an ornament on the shelf, yet the stillness left him unnerved. Time stretched as Garrett waited for news of his fiancée. Which one? Or both. What a state to find oneself in.

He'd seen Beverly conscious and breathing—due in no small part to Bessy's ministrations. For some reason he understood that so long as Beverly was in the care of Bessy's capable hands, she would be fine. In this area, Bessy gave off every confidence, as one most practiced in the skill of healing.

147

Still, he knew from the look on her face that she fretted. This reaction seemed a natural one with a treasured loved one being hurt or injured. She'd likely agonize until her sister regained her strength. While Garrett was concerned for Beverly, he felt the greater anxiety about Bessy's reaction to the day's events and what she'd heard, or thought she heard. The woman had been thunderous when they first marched toward the carriage.

His confidence was rewarded shortly after his arrival when the lady's maid reported his fiancée slept.

"Fitful, sir," she said, when he questioned her state. "But Mistress Anne assures she is in no further danger."

That had been some time ago. When he dallied without making a move to leave, as it seems she'd thought he would, she finally cast him a quizzical look, shrugged one shoulder, curtsied, and then left the room. Barely a breath later, the butler arrived to ask how he might make Garrett more comfortable. The pleasantry didn't mask the true intention of wondering what Garrett wanted by staying in a house where there was no entertainment to be had with all the family occupied by health concerns and other matters.

"I shall beg an audience with the master of the house when he is able."

"Would you not prefer to come back, sir?" the butler asked, spine rigid, hands right to his sides.

"No, Arthur. I would not." Garrett spoke with the command perfected through his captainship. The butler's rounded, wide-set eyes showed the desired effect. "There are matters of concern, and I will wait, if it pleases you."

"Yes, sir," the man said as he made to leave the

room by backing out, nodding. "As you wish. I will convey the message to Mister MacLeod."

"I'm sure you will," Garrett muttered under his breath as the door closed with the softness of a whisper.

Now that Beverly appeared in no mortal danger, Garrett prepared for the battle ahead. He knew Gerald would assume Garrett's father supported the notion, which he'd termed craziness when they last spoke. Had they not been interrupted by Bessy's untimely entrance, Garrett felt sure he would have won the man over. Loss of a battleground wasn't the position in which he wanted to start, but what choice did he have? The longer this went unresolved, the less likely a successful outcome.

With this lapse of time, Gerald could have spoken to his father, yet because he'd not been confronted, Garrett assumed he retained the upper hand. He would maintain his strategy of getting his way and only alerting Mackenzie once the deal was finalized. This was, after all, how their export enterprise had grown under Garrett these last years.

Circling the room, he paused in front of a miniature painting of the sisters. Their faces, each unique, had similarities he hadn't noticed before. They smiled at the painter as commanded, the pose unnatural, as all portraits appeared to Garrett. But there was a quiet between them, some bond that the artist had managed with his brush strokes. He did wonder how a painter who demanded hours of a person to hold still expected to capture the real person. Still, qualities of the siblings jumped out at him. Perhaps this was based on his own knowledge rather than some magic of the brush. Beverly's softened jaw, tipped by a pointed chin

149

belying her innate ability to get her way without the person ever knowing they gave in. Bessy's equally set jaw was counterbalanced with her wide brow and set, determined stare.

Garrett set the frame back in its position. This provided food for thought as he relived the day's events prior to Beverly's sting. Had that been what Beverly did to him earlier today in the garden? She had set about to get her own way through her natural guile. How he must have surprised her with his revelation. Garrett smiled. He hoped so.

He again studied the rendering, concentrating on his Bessy and scoffing at a sudden urge to pocket the small picture. There was a crinkle by her eyes suggesting Beverly had made her laugh. Her face tilted but her gaze was direct, uncompromising. The painter had highlighted a glint in their depths. He recognized this as authentic.

Garrett crooked a finger and his thumb to brush his stubble as he considered the pose. No, the artist hadn't taken liberties. The glint was definitely there. Perhaps it went unnoticed due to Bessy's mild ways in company not of her choosing, but he'd experienced it often enough, in the woods, at the party. And he wanted to see it more. He wanted to see her in a good fit of temper. He wondered what she looked like in the throes of passion. Yes, he wanted to be there for both and so much more.

He scanned the frame for the artist's name. He would like to hire this person for a larger portrait of his wife-to-be. Yes, he determined. She would be his wife.

Garrett traced the contours of the picture frame, then strode across the room. He would have his way. In this he was certain. Now that Beverly had confirmed her own feelings in the matter, Garrett saw the way clear and would no longer brook interference. If the families wanted an alliance, then they would allow Bessy and Garrett to unite. Otherwise...

Bessy's entrance into the room caused his reflections to cease, and he felt the hair rise along his arms. After her gaze met his, she quickly averted her face. However, her hung head did little to hide the scorched flush which blazed from her neck up. So, he mused, Beverly had told her of their plan.

Despite his planning, he hadn't imagined what he'd do if he got his own way. At a sudden loss, Garrett struggled with how to respond. He pushed his fists into his pockets. Was now the opportunity to declare himself, or should he wait for affirmation from Gerald first? His brain warred while he took a pace forward, changed his mind, and resumed his stance by the mantel clock.

"The Lady Beverly fares well?"

A long moment passed. He searched her stance, wishing he could glimpse her eyes. Would there be that glint pictured in her portrait? Would he be able to tell her thoughts? Her slight frame revealed nothing...but that scarlet coloring persisted. What did it mean?

Uncertainty squeezed his guts, and he again questioned whether to wait for a sign from Bessy before addressing the contract with her father. But he could not. With Beverly's plan fresh in his mind, he would proceed. If Bessy rejected him after, he would persuade the dissolution of the agreement, for he would not marry an unwilling woman, despite arrangements.

Bessy's gaze met his squarely but briefly before

lowering to her hands. "My sister—"

Gerald boomed into the room, seeming to take all the air necessary for her to continue.

Harriet trailed after, seeming to talk for the sake of chatter rather than to have anything meaningful to contribute. This was her way, as far as all of his encounters with the couple. He could not hold it against her, nor could he stand to be within her proximity for great lengths of time.

Gerald glanced from Bessy to him, and back again, stalled in the middle of the room. He placed his hands on his hips, and Garrett read the man's posture clearly. He was trying to gauge if he and Bessy had made an arrangement. Had circumstances been confirmed behind his back. How much of this debacle remained under his control.

Then he shook his head. "So, you're still here," Gerald said, nodding in Garrett's direction. "Arthur indicated you'd been apprised of my daughter's good fortune in her...ah...accident, yet stayed to discuss matters with me."

"Of course," Garrett replied, placing a forearm against the rock mantel and crossing one booted foot over the other. The fire in the grate burned low and didn't cast much warmth, which befit the chilly atmosphere permeating the room. He returned Gerald's gaze measure for measure. "The welfare of my future bride is foremost in my mind."

Gerald gaped at the intended double meaning and turned his head to regard his youngest child. "Anne has told you, then, that Beverly thrives," he said, acknowledging Bessy's presence for the first time. "For this miracle, I guess my younger daughter's many forays to the village healer have not been in vain."

Bessy's head lifted, and for the briefest of moments, she met Garrett's gaze. She stepped farther into the room. Color flared fresh, and a pain stabbed his heart at her discomposure. How he wished he could be forthright with her and avoid all this nonsensical protocol, be as they were as children...

"Certainly not in vain," Garrett agreed, peering at Bessy, who again lowered her head, refusing to speak for herself, despite moving forward another step. She no longer looked like a frightened bird ready to take flight, but a falcon identifying her prey.

"Healers are in short supply, I think you will agree," Garrett said, returning his stare to Gerald, feeling more confident. "A gift, really."

"Really?"

"I remain to continue our conversation," he said, striving to maintain a posture completely contrary to the raving storm of doubt in his heart. "A matter of utmost importance for the future. Mine, yours, and Bess—Anne's."

Gerald's gaze shifted from him to Bessy, then to Harriet. "I think there are better moments than now. Do you not agree?" he said. "For sure we've all had quite enough excitement, and matters such as these can wait for another day."

"Unfortunately, I have to respectfully disagree. The time has come where I must act on this contract, as I must return to my ship. Our business does not stop with the season. Duty calls, I'm afraid."

Gerald turned to face Bessy. "You may go, Anne," he said, pointing back to the door and the wide staircase beyond. "Your sister still needs you."

"No," came Bessy's simple, almost inaudible response.

"No?" Gerald thrust his hand back on his hip. "What has come over my household this last week?"

At this, Bessy lifted her head and faced her father. The determined line of her spine, flanked by the squaring off of her shoulders, hailed to their encounter in the woods. She would not be budged. "Beverly is fine for now. I will remain."

Apparently reading the same message in her posture as Garrett did, Gerald turned to him. "Surely a day will not matter—"

"I will have her." A male voice from the doorway boomed, announcing the ill-timed visit of Henry Rathmore.

Garrett almost laughed out loud at the dramatic timing.

Rathmore stepped to within a few feet of Gerald and pointed at Garrett. "I am equal to Garrett in wealth, prestige, and land holding. Plus I'm titled. This will not be a battle I will lose. I love Beverly and she me. And I will have her for my wife."

"Bloody hell," Gerald roared.

Harriet gasped and clapped a hand across her mouth. "Gerald."

Like an old bear, Gerald shook his head and pointed at all three of them. "Has this younger generation no respect for their elders?"

Chapter Nineteen

That she could have imagined such a moment! Just when she wished for Bevvy to be there to share it, she glanced back toward the staircase, and there stood her sister.

"Oh, my land," Harriet uttered, hands fanning her face. "What is the meaning of this?"

Anne felt him by her side before looking up and meeting the intensity of his dark blue gaze. Garrett smiled down at her, and then and only then did she know the truth of her sister's words. Abashed but buoyed by this knowledge, Anne forced herself to smile. He held out his hand, and without further encouragement, she laced her fingers in his.

Garrett nodded and moved them as a unit to face her father. "Gerald, with your permission, I would like to request permission to marry Anne."

"What?" Harriet exclaimed. "Oh!" she said and slumped to the chair.

"So you do know my name," Anne leaned in to whisper, unable to contain her smile.

Garrett lowered his head a fraction. "You will always be my Bessy, but on this formal occasion, I felt the need."

Garrett's words were drowned by Henry closing the distance from the door to the fireplace. "I will have…" Henry's words trailed as he glanced around the

155

room his narrow features blotched, his wavy hair wild. "You…and Anne?"

"Too much," Gerald yelled above the growing din and the servants gathering to take in the spectacle, wondering if they were needed. His face had turned a rather concerning shade of purple. "All too much! There is a contract."

"Yes, the contract," Beverly affirmed from the doorway, seeming to take no notice of her father's state. Her eyes darted with a dancing fire from Henry to her father, then to settle on Anne, a smile as she pointedly acknowledged their union of hands. Then she returned her calm gaze to her father. "As Garrett outlined, the contract will be fulfilled as mother intended. Our families united. Your daughters happy with their matches."

"Not as outlined—"

Losing her composure, Beverly rushed across the room and took her father's face between her palms. "Mother wanted her daughter to marry Flora's son. Two mothers—the very best of friends—sisters of the heart, wanting their families to be one." Bevvy's words gushed, urgent, intent, determined to have her father listen. "And she will have that. Don't you see? One of her daughters loves Martha's son. Look, Father. See, for once."

Beverly moved Gerald's face toward where Garrett and Anne stood. "See? They are a match," she said, stress evident in her weakened voice. "Better than Mother could ever have wished. Theirs will be a union of love, of respect. Look with your heart, Father. See, as Mother intended."

Beverly's pale face waxed whiter still as she stood,

gowned but barefooted. Beverly seemed to sway and reach for a hold. Anne made to rush to her sister's side before she fainted, but Henry was there before her.

With a hand to his beloved's side, holding her steady, he smiled broadly. "With respect, sir," Henry began, his deep baritone—his one redeeming feature in Anne's view—drawing their father's attention. "May I ask for your blessing in my proposal of a union between myself and your daughter Beverly?"

In that moment, Anne could see the attraction and love between her sister and the man she was almost forced to wed in her stead. Garrett's grip tightened upon her own, and she looked into his eyes and saw joy reflected there. How differently this all could have ended had her sister and this man not devised a solution. Her throat contracted as she imagined how close they had come to losing her beloved sister, to losing one another, four hearts shattered.

She lowered her gaze, embarrassed by her overwhelming emotion. Then Garrett's crooked finger was under her chin. He lifted her gaze to his. "No, my dear, do not hide from me ever again."

"This is…this is," Gerald spluttered, having taken a seat next to his wife, "all too much. We need time—"

"Good sir," Garrett said, stepping forward, positioning Anne's hand in the crook of his arm. "May I propose a joint wedding within a fortnight. This will allow for the banns and society announcements, and more importantly the fulfilment of the contract. All will celebrate your good fortune of happy alignments for your daughters and for your family's legacy."

****

Anne stared down at her hand freshly adorned and

twisted the ring around her finger. The weight of the golden band was both a comfort and a marvel. Wind whipped her skirts and dismantled the elaborate hairstyle Bevvy had so painstakingly assembled that morning. Anne had told her 'twould be a waste of effort, but her sister would not see her leaving her country, her home, destined for the new world and a new life with her husband, looking like a squire's urchin.

A tear rolled down Anne's face. She sorely missed her sister already. What would become of her in this new life? When Garrett had asked her to accompany him, she didn't hesitate. She understood how much the sea meant to him and how encouraging him to leave it behind would be like asking her to give up her healing, which he assured her he would never do. And so, like his parents before, they were setting out on their adventure together.

She would have a new home, he assured her, in Boston—a new life, a new start. One she could make her own. As much as she would miss her family, especially Beverly, the fizzle of excitement chased the loneliness away.

"Say it again." A voice whispered in her ear, sending a shiver of recognition down her spine. The memory of their wedding night caused her stomach to spiral and heat to flood every inch of her body. Had she but known…

She lowered her head to gaze at the railing. The familiar fingers crooked and lifted her chin. This had been his chant throughout a night filled with love and first experiences. Every time she reached new heights, he'd ask her to say it. "I will," she responded. Like she had when the vicar recited the vows.

Would she take this man as her husband? "I will."

Would she be true in good times and in bad? "I will."

Will you promise to love and honor all the days of your life? "I will."

When Garrett asked her in their marriage bed if she would be his lover, his wife, the mother of his children? "I will."

When he stroked her body like a newly strung instrument and asked her if she would allow him to make love to her? She gasped, "I will."

"Will you love me forever, as I love you?" he asked staring deeply into her eyes, she answered, vision blurred by tears of happiness. "I will."

And now, a sneak peek into Book Three of the McGuire Series:

Backlash Bounty

by

Lori Power

Chapter One

1813 Capraia Isola

Garrett McGuire straightened and stretched his back. The creaks and cracks offered a welcomed relief from the toil. He took the bandana from his neck and mopped his streaming brow. Strands of his hair had come loose and clung to his face.

Members of his crew, stooped from their combined labor, followed his lead. They rested in various poses, wiping blood and sweat on trouser legs and arms of their shirts.

He glanced down at his own sea-hardened hands, bloodied from the volcanic rocks blocking the cavern they wished to expose. They had wrapped their hands with strips of leather to protect as much as they could, but the barrier created little armor. The razor-like edges sliced shallow seams through the callouses. The fluid pearled but didn't run.

First Mate Brian MacLeod, brother to his beloved wife, Bessy, leaned a shoulder against the boulder and pierced him with a knowing stare, then nodded. MacLeod swiped the rag from his head to wipe the rillettes of perspiration. Garrett noted the normally light brown hair appeared near black with the damp. The man re-tied his bandana and smiled at Garrett, revealing a gap in the crooked array of teeth. "Does this mean we're officially pirates now, Capt'in?"

Garrett arched his arms high above his head and rolled his neck first one way and then the other. Squinting against the glare of the sun, he looked out over the small harbor where his ship, the *Isle Sky*, bobbed at anchor while he contemplated his answer. The island of Elba lay just visible as a purple streak on the horizon.

The mention of "pirate" grazed a nerve, and not a pleasurable one at that. The pursuit of treasure had started his family's legacy when his father first uncovered the loot from Oak Island. Though many might guess, they had never confirmed the rumors, nor did he intend ever to reveal the family secret. This kind of notoriety was something he would prefer not to carry in the normal course of business.

Still, Garrett found an easy smile and shook his head. "No." He stretched the word, feeling for the length of their voyage they'd been on a fool's errand. Despite their friendship and being a brother by marriage, Garrett would not confirm what Brian presumed.

At this point, for this task, Brian knew all. How much to reveal openly to the crew at large would depend on what they found. To come so far without booty for payment wouldn't make for happy men. They were well used to a percentage of all they bartered between the two sides. There was no need for decision now. He'd consider what to do about that later.

"No," he repeated. "This 'ere's British soil. Been so since '96 under Admiral Nelson. Today we work to his majesty's pleasure."

Though the directions to the island had been received covertly, care of Cornwallis out of Halifax, they were clear and precise. What might amount to nothing required inspecting to be sure. He had been so entrusted because he'd been running successful clandestine trade operations for the last eighteen months, alternating between the British and those fledging Americans. Who would win wouldn't be determined by him. His task was to ensure he and his men, his business interests, were well placed for either outcome.

His gaze traveled the length of the rocky beach, then scanned the horizon for a telltale mast. The last thing he needed now was competition or discovery. Weariness had become a faithful friend on this mission. By its very nature, standing outside their normal merchant activities, this consignment was very different. Even though he knew Cornwallis had assigned this mission based on the rumors of his father, still he had no confidence in the outcome. The age of the map, the location of the island, the fact that the Admiral clearly had never found what he and his crew now sought troubled Garrett as no other assignment had before.

His men, loyal and well-paid, followed him without question, MacLeod being his only confidant to the extent of what they sought. Spanish treasure. He certainly had no allegiance to anything Spanish and took great personal joy in outstripping them of any bounty, whatever that may be. He shook his head at the incredulity of the very notion. Something whispered in his doubting mind that surely all treasure worth finding had already been found.

"Not so much pleasure today," MacLeod replied, curling a length of rope over his arm. "'Tis a lonesome island, to be sure. Not fit for man, barely survivable by the few beasts hereabouts. Whatever they think might be here—"

Garrett clamped a hand on the man's upper arm. "Waste of time, I'm sure, MacLeod." He lowered his voice, then winked. "Nor do I think our sovereign expects anything. But war is expensive, my friend. Finding this before Napoleon will either alter the course or confirm the old abbot was as crazy as his jailers suspected."

"Big risk for a waste of time," said Ruddy Roddy, one of the ten trusted men he'd allowed to come ashore. He sat close enough to hear the first but not the last of Garrett's comments. "I sees Italy. If we're not on our way with the next tide, we're sure to be spotted by the Frenchies patrolling from Marseille."

"On that I can agree," said Garrett, reaching for the rope dangling from MacLeod's thick forearm. "Best to be done and on our way, eh, men?"

With murmured groans but no complaints, they rose and re-formed their two groups. While the men worked the lever under the boulder, he and MacLeod pushed the rope around the edges. The wild goats, which had scattered at their arrival, had returned to their grazing, seemingly no longer viewing the seamen as a threat. He smiled at this. The periodic bleats reminded Garrett that, if nothing else, they'd have fresh meat for their efforts.

"Be lively, lads," he encouraged.

He and MacLeod criss-crossed the rope around the

back of the rock. "Okay, that'll do for a moment," he commanded. "Now to the ropes."

Leaving the lengths of cord in place, they dug deep beneath the stone. The two lines formed along each end of the rope and began to heave until they felt the great weight give way. Though it may only have been fractional, it was enough to re-energize their efforts.

"To the top now, Spider." Garrett shouted to the wiry dwarf-like man who, on a normal day at sea, could scale a mainsail mast like an insect. "Use your legs and push."

Encouraged by the sudden movement of the great weight, they worked as a unit until the mass rolled from its historic foundation a few inches along the jimmies.

"Heave," MacLeod bellowed. "Put yur backs into it."

"I can see inside," Spider yelled.

"Enough," Garrett bawled. "Stay as you are. Hold tight. Don't let this massive bastard retake its hold in the foundation." He turned to Ruddy Roddy. "The light. Quick, man."

The young man scrambled away and returned just as quickly with the lantern, already lit.

The skin of Garrett's bare back tore as he squeezed his large form through the narrow entrance. Although he winced, he didn't pause. Stale air, damp and aged, filled his lungs. Here was a grave if ever there was.

MacLeod followed, pushing at the immovable mass to lever his wide shoulders within. "Hold this burly piece of Mother Earth, boys. It'll not make me day to be trapped inside," he shouted back to the men before dipping his head to clear the small opening, a rush torch in his outstretched hand.

With just the two of them in the cavern, Garrett laid the oil lamp on the damp stone at his feet and stooped to retrieve the ancient map from his boot. His stomach clenched. The entrance was exactly as the map described. "Three paces from where the teeth mesh."

"What could that mean?" MacLeod stood to peer around.

Garrett lifted the light and glanced around the claustrophobic interior. Then his breath sailed from his body and he felt almost giddy. "There, MacLeod." He pointed along the length of wall, observing the cave wasn't nearly as small as he'd first thought. He was again the small boy who stole into the secret vault of their family to be dazzled by the jewels contained therein.

Measuring his step, he strode the length of wall that unless inspected properly looked as though it were the end. Up close however, stalagmites met stalactites as teeth along a jawline. Retrieving the light, he felt between the white columns, pushing until one broke and he could wedge his way into the mouth.

Water sloshed above the top off his boot. "More light."

MacLeod held the torch aloft while he followed through the gnashing jaws of rock. The sudden light in the gloom gave Garrett a wide view of what lay within and what would have been missed had they not had the map.

"By the Lord Jesus, this will end 'er."

A word about the author…

Turning passion into words in print is a dream come true for Lori Power.

From radio host (best job ever!), DJ, news reporter to newspaper journalist, like many authors, Lori has been writing most of her life.

In writing, Lori has discovered a truism: everyone has a great story to tell. All you need to do is listen. Over the years, with all the people Lori has met previously and meets daily, both professionally and personally, with an ear to the ground, readers can often find these 'characters' fictionalized in stories.

Not confined to one genre, Lori has published select children's books and one cookbook, based on a gluten-free diet, as well as non-fiction industry blogs.

Lori's first novel, *Storms of Passion*, was published by The Wild Rose Press under their Champagne line in 2014. Her second novel, *Hit 'n Run*, book 1 in the "Under Suspicion" series, was published by Limitless Press in 2015.

Collaboration is important to improving one's craft, and as such, Lori is an active member of the TransCanada Romance Writers, Romance Writers of America, and The Alberta Romance Writers Association, and belongs to both a critiquing group and a Beta Reading weekly group.

Lori looks forward to continuing to find the good story, hashing out a scene, having fun with a character, and writing the story she would love to read.

www.marinerwrites.com

Thank you for purchasing
this publication of The Wild Rose Press, Inc.

For questions or more information
contact us at
info@thewildrosepress.com.

The Wild Rose Press, Inc.
www.thewildrosepress.com